BLACK LEGION

Something sinister is taking place in the Sahara. The inhabitants of an Arab village are carried away to slavery; then Fort Allengrah, a French Foreign Legion base, disappears from the face of the earth along with its inhabitants. Captain Hugh Radford, a British special agent working with Interpol, is given a temporary commission in the Foreign Legion, with an American airman and a French ballistics expert. Outnumbered, cut off from help, and almost unarmed, Radford and his two companions must fight to save the whole free world . . .

JOHN ROBB

BLACK LEGION

Complete and Unabridged

LINFORD
Leicester

First published in Great Britain

First Linford Edition
published 2020

*A catalogue record for this book is available
from the British Library.*

ISBN 978–1–4448–4446–7

1

Doomed Village

Panting for breath, the old Arab crawled to the crest of a dune. Then he saw Fort Allengrah. From his parched lips came a faint croaking sound. Taiba, headman of the village of Gacruss, was uttering words of thanks.

It was far away, that fort. The Tricolour of France, flapping lazily over the compound buildings, was a mere speck. So were the figures of the legionnaires who were patrolling the red stone ramparts. Perhaps they were too far away . . .

Eleven days had passed since the terror at Gacruss. Days during which Taiba had walked, limped and finally crawled across two hundred miles of desert. He had been able to drink at the occasional water holes. For food, there had been a slab of goat meat which he had begged with difficulty from a group of passing Tuareg tribesmen.

Now at last, with Fort Allengrah before him, he would be able to demand vengeance. When he told of the crime against his people, the Legion garrison would surely act immediately.

Taiba raised a scrawny hand and waved it. At the same time, a ghastly thought came to him. Suppose those sentries did not see him? If that happened, he would certainly die where he lay. For Taiba knew that the last of his strength was gone. He could not move another yard.

It was a vulture which did it. It was one of those evil-eyed and ugly birds which saved the life of Taiba. It had been circling over the fort, squawking and hoping to snatch up some morsel of waste food. Then suddenly it sped out over the sand, alighting in a distant dune. There it remained — very still, shaggy wings outstretched. The sentry on the southern ramparts watched it with mild interest, or obviously the bird was waiting for the moment when it would be safe to strike at newly found prey.

But what was the prey?

The sentry pulled his *kepi* well over his eyes, shading them from the heat glare.

Abruptly, he tensed, fixing his gaze at a point where something was moving. It looked like an Arab's *burnous*.

Quickly, the legionnaire unslung his Lebel. He tapped the heel of the butt against the ramparts in a signal to the sergeant of the guard. After a few moments, the sergeant emerged from the guard-room, which was just within the massive gates. He blinked in the sudden light as he looked to the top of the south wall.

'What is it, legionnaire?'

'There's an Arab out there,' the sentry said, pointing. 'He looks as if he's in serious trouble.'

The sergeant was pulling a pair of field-glasses from their leather case as he mounted the thirty steps to the ramparts.

Three minutes later the gates were being unbarred. Creaking, they were dragged open. And, throwing up sprays of sand, a light armoured car sped towards that dune.

★   ★   ★

Major Callise, officer commanding Fort Allengrah, looked up from his desk work as the medical officer entered.

'Well?' he asked. 'Is the old Arab going to recover?'

The medical officer nodded. 'I think so. He's suffering very badly from exposure and exhaustion, but he's tough. Some men don't die easily and he's one of them. However . . . ' The medical officer hesitated, then went on: 'I think he's gone mad.'

'I daresay he has. No one can wander about the desert for days without running that risk. I suppose he'll get over it?'

'I suppose he will. The trouble is that in every way he *seems* sane enough, except that he talks such nonsense.'

'What sort of nonsense?' Major Callise asked without a lot of interest.

'He says that legionnaires have surrounded his village, shot two of the people there and taken all the others away to forced labour.'

Major Callise was holding a silver pencil. He let it clatter on to his desk. 'Repeat that,' he said after a long pause. The medical officer did so. 'Clearly, he is mad,' Major Callise muttered when he had finished.

'He insists on seeing you.'

'Why should I see a man who's taken leave of his senses? It'd be wasting my time and his.'

'I agree, but this man must have complete rest — and I don't think he'll relax until he has spoken to you.'

With a weary sigh, Major Callise stood up. 'I'd better hear his story if he takes it as seriously as that,' he said.

The two officers walked briskly towards the fort's sick bay. When they entered the whitewashed room, a fragile figure struggled feebly to reach a sitting position. Very gently, the medical officer pressed him back on to the bed.

'No need to get excited,' he told Taiba. 'Major Callise is here and he's ready to hear your story.'

Taiba turned his heavy bloodshot eyes until they were focusing on the major. 'You . . . you command this fort?' he asked in little more than a whisper.

The Arabic dialect was familiar to Major Callise. He replied in the same tongue. 'I do — and I'm glad we found you in time. You've had a bad experience and I believe you want to tell me about it.'

There was a long silence. It ended when Taiba gasped: 'We Algerians . . . are we not also French?'

If Major Callise was surprised by the question, he did not show it. He nodded. 'Certainly. All Algerians, no matter what the colour of their skin, are also full citizens of France.'

'Then answer this — have we, the people of Gacruss, ever been disloyal to France? Have we not always been your friends?'

'Certainly, but . . . '

'Then why did your legionnaires come to our village with the dawn to force its people in slavery? Why did they slay with pistol bullets two of our young men who had the courage to resist?'

'You are ill, Taiba. The sickness makes you imagine things which cannot be true. But soon you'll be well, then — '

'But I tell you that I speak only the truth!' There was sudden wild strength in Taiba's voice and he tried once again to raise himself. 'I saw all with my own eyes!

Two score men of the Legion descended upon us. They made us gather in our marketplace. They said they had work for us.'

'Where were you supposed to do this work, Taiba?'

'They did not tell us. They only said that it was many miles away. I, as the headman, spoke to their officer. I told him he could not do this thing. He struck me and I fell. Two of our young men rushed at the officer, for they could not see me treated thus. The officer shot them with his pistol, even as dogs are shot. I saw all that.'

Major Callise examined the tip of his cane thoughtfully as he asked: 'Who was this officer?'

'How could I know? For I'd never seen him before. He wore the badges of a colonel.'

'Very well. Then what happened?'

'The rest of the people were now afraid — very afraid. They were allowed to collect food and some water from our well. Then they were marched away to the south and Gacruss was left deserted.'

'But how about you? Why did they allow you to go free?'

Taiba fluttered a trembling hand. 'I heard the officer say that I was too old for work and not worth a bullet. Without my people to tend to me, I'd die anyway in a few days, he said. So they left me. They did not know that the strength of a man is in his heart as much as in his body. And I, Taiba, am wise in the ways of the desert. So I resolved that above all else I must reach this fort and ask why your legionnaires did this to us.'

A battery-driven cooling fan was spinning near Taiba's bed. Major Callise moved towards it. He stood in the airstream, mopping his face and gazing at the Arab. Several times his lips parted as if he were about to speak, but no sound emerged. At last he said: 'It's all quite impossible.'

'The truth cannot be impossible!'

'So you say.' Then, in a more kindly voice he added: 'An investigation will be made at once. Meantime, try to rest.'

'I have always trusted the French,' Taiba whispered, closing his eyes. 'Even now I have not lost faith, for I know that justice will be done.'

Back in his office, Major Callise sent for his adjutant. He repeated Taiba's story, while blank astonishment spread over the adjutant's face.

'He *must* have taken leave of his senses,' Major Callise concluded. 'Anyway, Gacruss is in this military area, so if legionnaires had been sent then we would know about it.'

'What are you going to do?' the adjutant asked

'I'm sending out a patrol immediately. A sergeant and six men in one of the armoured cars ought to be enough. See to that for me — and tell the patrol to send me a radio report just as soon as they've had a look at the village.'

* * *

Four days later . . .

The tall and elegantly clothed figure of Captain Hugh Radford sauntered out of Interpol headquarters in Paris. He paused on the pavement to sniff the June air and to flick an almost invisible speck of dust from his grey Savile Row suit. Then his lean, pleasant face broke into a smile as he approached an official car which was waiting for him.

'A glorious day,' he said to the driver. 'Much too pleasant for work. Still, there's work to be done, so we can make a start by going to the Defence Ministry.'

Radford settled in the back seat. As the car swung into the line of traffic he opened a briefcase which lay on his lap. He drew out half a dozen typewritten sheets. They were marked *Secret — Schedule A*. And they told a baffling, almost incredible story. Glancing through the pages, Radford reminded himself of the main points.

The first hint of trouble had come a month ago. Frightened tribesmen who had been crossing the lonely Asben Plateau region of the Sahara Desert fled to the small oasis town of Batak. There they told the resident commissioner that they had been chased by 'great birds of prey which roared like thunder in the night.'

It soon became obvious that they must — for the first time in their lives — have seen aircraft.

But the territory was far from any airline route. And no French military planes had been anywhere near it. So the commissioner put in a report to Algiers which was forwarded to Paris. There no one took it very seriously and it was soon forgotten. But not for long.

Two weeks passed. Then the same commissioner, a M. Renoir, heard of a new story which was sweeping through the marketplaces of Batak. This time, Arabs were whispering that 'giant guns' were being erected in the foothills of the Asben Plateau. But it proved impossible to find anyone who had seen such guns.

M. Renoir put in another report.

By now the French government was becoming worried. They were certainly not installing any artillery there. It would be useless to do so, for there was nothing to defend in the region and nothing to attack.

A squadron of long-distance bombers was ordered to fly out from Oran to look at the plateau. They saw nothing — nothing save the sand and gaunt rocks which rose in jagged hills to make one of the most remote and forbidding places on earth

The government relaxed again. But again it was not for long. Now had come by far the most serious blow. Fort Allengrah, which was about two hundred and fifty miles north of the plateau, had received the staggering information that the entire population of an Arab village named Gacruss had been abducted by men in Legion uniform.

A patrol had been sent out. They had found the place entirely deserted of human life.

But that was not all.

They had also found the bodies of two young Arabs. They had been shot. And that supported story that they were murdered while resisting the captors.

That was how the matter stood. As he considered the facts, Radford's face changed. Gone was his normal easy-going and slightly lazy expression, which had misled so many people. His blue eyes were hard. So, too, was the set of his mouth and jaw.

He thought: *There's an answer to all this and it's got to be found. But right now I'm darned I can even make a guess at it. It looks like the toughest case I've ever handled.*

But was it his case? He realised that he could not even be sure of that. True, he was a special agent attached to the British Bureau of the International Police headquarters. But this did not look like an Interpol matter. Yet he had been given urgent orders to read the file then report to General Phillipe, Deputy Chief of the French General Staff.

'Anyway, I'll soon know the answer to that one,' Radford told himself as the car stopped in the courtyard of the Defence Ministry.

Two minutes later he was being shown into the room of General Phillipe, a tall grey-haired soldier. They shook hands, then Red sat opposite him.

'You have studied the facts?' General Phillipe asked.

'Yes, sir. It all seems . . . well, it seems fantastic.'

'It *is* fantastic, *Capitaine* Radford. Most of it may be put aside as wild rumour. But the village of Gacruss — *ciel!* That cannot be forgotten so easily.'

Radford asked: 'Has any theory been put forward as to why the place was deserted and why two Arabs were found shot?'

The general shrugged his shoulders. 'Theories! There have been plenty of them, but none bears a moment's examination. We are left with the possibility that the story told by Taiba, the headman of Gacruss, is true.'

'But it just cannot be entirely true. We know that legionnaires were not responsible.'

'*Oui.* So where does that get us?'

'It gets us to the point where we must accept that men in Legion uniforms who were *not* legionnaires abducted the Arabs,' Radford said softly.

'Exactly! The more we think about it, the more of a nightmare it all becomes. Where would such men come from? And how would they arrive? By air perhaps? But even so, why would they want to go into the Asben region? That Arab headman said that his people were taken away for forced labour. Yet what sort of labour would be of any use to anyone in that forsaken territory?'

A large scale wall-map hung behind the general. He rose and moved towards it. Red followed.

'The plateau is part of an immense wedge of higher ground which stretches for nearly two thousand miles from east to west across the Sahara,' he went on, pointing with a forefinger. 'Among the rocks and chasms, whole armies could hide without being seen by our planes. Little wonder, then, that our airmen saw nothing unusual. It would be even more useless to attempt a search from the ground. To do the job properly would need every soldier in Europe and, even so, it would be next to impossible to keep them supplied with food and water. Do you see what I'm getting at?'

'I think so, sir,' Radford said. 'You're satisfied that *something* very peculiar is happening, but before you can do anything you must know exactly where look.'

'Precisely,' General Phillipe said, giving a quick smile. 'Once we know that, we will move fast and we'll hit hard.'

'So that's why the problem has been handed to Interpol?'

'*Oui.* Interpol must hand us the exact information we want. After that, the Legion and the Air Force will take over.'

Radford hesitated. Then he asked: 'You have your own intelligence department. Wouldn't it be better if they handled this? Surely they'd be more . . . '

General Phillipe held up a hand and shook his head.

'These inquiries must be made very quietly,' he said. 'We do not want to put our enemies — whoever they may be — on their guard. Our own army agents would probably do just that because they are all Frenchmen. But you, being British, will be much less likely to create suspicion. We've had a careful look at your dossier, *Capitaine*, and we are satisfied that you are the officer for this task. You have had an outstanding record with Interpol and you also speak several Arabic dialects quite fluently.'

Radford strolled back to his chair. 'When and how do I begin?' he asked.

'It has been arranged that you will take an immediate commission in the Foreign Legion. Tonight you will fly to Oran, in

Algeria. From there, another plane will take you to Fort Allengrah, where you'll be able to talk to this Arab headman. He is your only lead at the moment. Major Callise, the commanding officer, knows what you are doing and who you really are. So do four men on our headquarters staff. To everyone else, you will simply be *Capitaine* Radford, a British-born officer of the Legion, who has been attached to Fort Allengrah on a map-making survey.'

General Phillipe opened a drawer, pulled out a large envelope and gave it to Red. 'This contains instructions for passing on any information you may get,' he continued. 'You'll also find in it a list of emergency contacts in Algeria — people who will help you if things look really serious. I want you to memorise them all, then destroy the — '

He broke off. The door had opened and a military aide had entered the room, holding a sheet of buff-coloured paper. The general said sharply: 'I gave orders that I was not to be interrupted!'

The aide swallowed nervously. 'I'm very sorry, *mon generale*, but this message has just arrived. You must see it immediately — it's vitally important.'

General Phillipe took the paper from him. As he read it, a strange change came over his face. The lines on it deepened. He became pale, almost ashen grey. And when at last he spoke, his voice had suddenly become old and tired. It was the voice of a man under severe shock.

'*Capitaine* Radford,' he said, 'you . . . you'll not be able to report to Fort Allengrah.'

'I won't? Why not?'

'Eleven hours ago, the fort ceased to send out its routine radio signals to head-quarters.'

The general gripped the edge of his desk, his voice fading away. Puzzled, Red moved towards him. 'Go on, sir. I'm listening.'

'At first it was thought that their transmitter must have broken down, and . . . '

'Yes — then what?'

'No one was very worried. But after a time it was decided to fly a plane over the fort with spare radio equipment which they could drop by parachute. But . . . but our airmen could not carry out that mission!'

'Couldn't! Why not?'

'Because Fort Allengrah is no longer there! It has vanished. The airmen found just a heap of rubble where the fort once stood!'

2

Terror from the Sky

A helicopter droned southwards. It was suspended between the pitiless Sahara sky and the searing wilderness of ever-shifting sand. Two men were in the machine and one of them was Radford. He was dozing in a passenger seat at the side of the pilot. His mind was flittering over the mass of events since, less than twenty-four hours ago, he had heard the staggering news of Fort Allengrah.

First, he had been transformed into a Legion officer. Identification papers had been supplied by the Records Department of the Defence Ministry. And he had been rushed to a military tailor in the fashionable Faubourg St. Honore, and fitted with uniform and equipment. The khaki drill tunic and slacks were similar to a British officer's kit. Only the high-crowned *kepi* was unfamiliar.

A civil airliner had swept him through the night from Paris to Oran, and then to Legion headquarters at Sidi bel Abbes. In the ancient town of Abbes, on the northern fringe of the Sahara, he had reported immediately to the general officer commanding. There, too, no time was being wasted.

'It's all grotesque,' the G.O.C. had told Radford. 'And the danger is beyond all description! If it becomes generally known that our forts can be wiped out at will, and villages seized without our knowing how or why, then all confidence in us will disappear. You know that we are making nuclear tests in the desert. That has already caused some anxiety. This as well, sacré! It could cause chaos in the whole Near and Middle East.'

Radford knew that the G.O.C. was not exaggerating. Britain and America, as well as France, had military bases in North Africa. They were a vital link in the defence of the free world. Their existence depended largely on the goodwill of the Arab peoples. That goodwill could switch to panic and hatred. Within days, the whole of the East might be aflame.

'We're doing our best to keep it quiet for as long as possible,' the officer had added. 'But soon the newspapers of the world will be bound to hear rumours. Before that happens, we *must* have solved the mystery and removed the danger.

'A team of ballistics experts have already been flown to ... to the site where Fort Allengrah once stood,' he continued. 'They are making a detailed examination and we await their first reports. It happens that ordinary aircraft can't land in the area so we are having to use helicopters. We have very few of these machines, so the Americans have placed several at our disposal. One of them is waiting fly you there now.'

So Radford had met Lieutenant Peter Largan, of the United States Army Air Force, who now sat at his side, piloting the long-range helicopter. They had taken a liking to each other from the moment they met. Radford found something reassuring about the squat bull-shouldered American, with the easy smile and the musical drawl of his native Texas. That voice of Peter's came to Radford now, breaking into his thoughts.

'Say, what made an English guy like you take a commission in the Legion?' he was asking. 'Were you tired of life?'

Radford did not want to lie to his newly found friend. But he certainly could not tell the truth. He evaded the question.

'Just one of those things,' Radford said.

'It's a tough life, isn't it? Do you like it?'

'I've nothing against it.'

'How long have you been in the outfit?'

'Not so long — how far now before we get to Fort Allengrah?'

'You mean, before we get to where the fort used to be! It ought to come in sight most any time, unless I've been given a wrong map reference. Know something? I sure wouldn't like to get myself lost over this desert. Nothing here except a whole lot of sand and rocks.'

'You must have been surprised when you were drafted to help us out,' Radford said, trying to keep the conversation away from himself.

'Yeah — but it makes a change.' Peter groped inside his leather flying-jacket and produced a packet of cigarettes. He was about to light one when he stiffened slightly at the controls, then pointed through the perspex cabin towards the horizon. 'Looks like we've almost arrived.'

A smudge on the sand was getting rapidly closer as Peter feathered the main prop to lose height. Radford took a pair of field-glasses from the leather case which was slung over his shoulder. Through it, he had his first look at what had been Fort Allengrah. A hiss of astonishment escaped through his teeth.

There was an enormous crater in the sand. It looked as if it had been scooped out by giant shovels. In the centre, it seemed to be all of thirty feet deep, and it formed a circle of at least two hundred yards diameter. Around the edges of it, Radford counted seven helicopters. They had been used to carry the ballistics experts who were examining the ground. Most of them were in the crater. Others were setting up what appeared to be scientific instruments on the edges. A few were huddled together in conference.

Bomber planes had already parachuted

stores to the party, and these had been assembled into piles some distance away.

'It looks even grimmer than I expected,' Radford said, putting the field-glasses away.

By now, they were directly over the site. Peter was bringing the helicopter down vertically. They landed near where the stores were assembled. Radford unbuckled his safety strap while Peter let down the exit ladder. As they got out of the machine, four men approached them. Three were in French uniform, the other a civilian. It was the civilian who spoke.

'I suppose you're Captain Radford. I'm Tiere — Professor Tiere. I've been sent out here because they had an idea that I could explain what's happened. I've been told to give you every co-operation.'

They shook hands and Radford introduced Peter. Then Radford asked: '*Do you know what's happened?*'

'I think so — the fort has been demolished by guided missiles.'

There was a long silence, during which Radford and Peter stared at each other.

'What makes you think that, Professor?'

Professor Tiere was a plump little man

and he was sweating freely. He unclipped his pince-nez glasses from his snub nose and gestured with them towards the crater.

'I have found fragments — only very tiny fragments — which look as if they have been part of rocket casings. In my opinion, more than one rocket landed directly on the fort.'

'You — you don't mean rockets with nuclear warheads?'

'*Sacre, non!* If that had been so, we'd not have been able to approach the area for days because of radiation. As it is, there's no sign of excessive radioactivity.'

'You're sure of that?'

'*Oui.* We tested with geiger counters before landing and after. Be assured that the warheads were filled with an orthodox explosive. Judging by the smell which still lingers, I'd say it was one of the nitro-derivatives. They have a terrible shattering effect — as you perhaps know.'

'Yes, I know,' Radford said. He advanced to the edge of the crater and looked into it. It was clear that Fort Allengrah, like most desert posts, had been built of red sandstone. This gave good protection against small arms fire, but it would shatter like glass under direct hits by H.E. rockets. Furthermore, the ammunition stored in the fort would add to the devastation.

Here and there, fragments of fort furnishing and equipment were recognisable. Radford saw a long sliver of brown wood which almost certainly had been part of a rifle butt. At the opposite side of the crater there were piles of weirdly twisted iron. They had been beds in which legionnaires had slept.

'I don't suppose anyone's survived?' Radford asked, half to himself.

'*Capitaine*, the age for that sort of miracle is long past,' the professor retorted just a little primly. 'Nothing made of flesh and blood could have lived. But we can be thankful for one thing — the garrison can't have known anything about it. One second, they'd be alive and well. Then — *boom!* — and they'd be dead.'

Peter, who had begun talking to one of the other helicopter pilots, suddenly shouted: 'Hey, Hugh! Looks like we've got visitors!'

Five horsemen were approaching at a slow canter. They had been concealed by dunes. Now, fully visible, they were no more than a quarter of a mile away. There was something awe-inspiring about those horsemen. Each was well over six feet high and they sat in their saddles with the erect dignity of statues. The lower part of their faces was covered by grey material. Their flowing robes were of the same cloth. As they came closer, it could be seen that their skin was shades fairer than one would expect of Arabs. And two of them had blue eyes.

'They're Tuaregs,' Radford said.

Peter had moved closer to Radford. 'Tuaregs? I guess they must be a tribe of Arabs?' he said.

Radford shook his head. 'They don't think of themselves as Arabs. They're pretty well a race apart. They have a terrific reputation as warriors and some people believe that they have a lot of white blood in them, which could account for their light skins.'

'White blood! How come?'

'It goes back hundreds of years — to

the Crusades, in fact. There's a theory that Tuaregs captured some of the crusaders who were going to the Holy Land and they intermarried. Some explorers have even reported seeing the warriors carrying swords and shields of a type which must have been made in Europe during the Middle Ages.'

There was no time for Radford to give any more facts about those people, for the five horsemen were within earshot. They reined in, staring first at the crater then at the men who were in and around it.

Professor Tiere was showing signs of feeling uneasy. He said to Radford: 'I'd like to know what they want. Can you speak their tongue?'

Radford nodded. 'They use a Berber dialect. I know it quite well.'

Before he could say any more, the Tuareg in the centre kneed his horse a little farther forward. He was even taller than his companions and he was one of the two whose eyes were blue.

'Is it that the earth has swallowed Fort Allengrah?' he asked.

Radford decided that nothing would be

gained by trying to play down the disaster. 'The fort has been destroyed,' he said, 'by our enemies.'

The Tuareg inclined his head in agreement. 'Your enemies strike from the sky. They are not men, such as you and I. They are of the heavens. You have angered the spirits, so your people perish.'

Radford caught his breath. 'You say our enemies come from the sky?'

'It is so.'

'How can you know that?'

'We know it because we saw it with our eyes. Two nights ago, great swords of fire travelled through the sky. They descended upon the fort of France. We saw it, I say.'

Quickly, Radford turned to the professor and translated the Tuareg's words. Professor Tiere's plump face creased with excitement.

'Fire in the sky! They'd be the rockets! I knew I was right. Ask him where they seemed to be coming from!'

Radford put the question. The Tuareg turned in his saddle and pointed to the south, towards the area of the Asben Plateau.

By now, more than a dozen Legion officers had joined the group. They were listening, fascinated.

'And we're back again to the plateau,' Radford said.

'See if you can get any more information,' Professor Tiere suggested.

Radford spoke for another couple of minutes with the Tuaregs. Then he said: 'We can't get any more from them because they've nothing to give. It seems that they were badly scared by what they saw the other night, which is natural enough. But curiosity brought them here today.' He paused, then added: 'I think it'd be a good idea to take a close look at that plateau.'

Professor Tiere shrugged. 'Aircraft have already surveyed it. They saw nothing.'

'I know. But a helicopter can be a lot more useful for that sort of work than ordinary planes.'

'*Mon ami* — the plateau is enormous! You will only be able to inspect a tiny part of it!'

'Better to inspect a tiny part than none at all. But I have a theory that the rocket launching area is not so far away.'

Peter moved forward. He said: 'I won't have enough fuel to get back to Sidi bel Abbes if we start jaunting over the plateau.'

'Fuel's been landed by parachute,' Red told him.

'We can fill the tanks now and get right off. We ought to be back here before dark.'

Professor Tiere hesitated, then he said: 'In that case, I think I will join you.'

They set to work to refuel the helicopter from the mass of four-gallon jerricans which had been dropped by parachute.

Half an hour later, they were rising over the crater. Red and the professor looked down at the upturned faces, which were getting rapidly smaller. At the other helicopters which remained on the ground. At the five Tuaregs, who were now riding away, determined not to be near the site of Fort Allengrah when darkness came.

'Hold steady at two thousand feet,' Radford told Peter. 'I want to let them know at headquarters what we're doing. At that altitude they ought to receive our radio loud and clear.'

'You're okay,' Peter said after a few

moments. 'You can start sending. We're holding the altitude steady at . . . '

The words died in his throat. He froze still. All of them froze still.

A streak of light was hurtling towards them. White, glaring light, travelling at an incredible speed from the area of the plateau. A vapour trail showed that it had first moved upwards in a great arc. Now it was descending — seeming to be coming straight for the helicopter.

'It's a rocket! A rocket . . . ' The professor's voice was pitched to a scream. But it was partly drowned by the hollow ghost-like shriek of the missile.

Falling, it passed directly in front of the helicopter. It passed so close that the air turbulence made the machine rock. But that was no more than a trivial foretaste.

In almost the same moment, the helicopter spun like a top. Then it reared up, as though it had been kicked from beneath by a giant boot. Because they had already unfastened their safety straps, Radford and Professor Tiere were thrown to the floor. Only Peter, holding frantically to his controls, managed to stay in his seat.

And a new sound reverberated in their ears. It was the tearing, evil crash of a detonating high explosive.

The men who had been working amid the ruins of Fort Allengrah were being murdered by rocket attack.

3

The Menacing Plateau

They were paralysed with horror. Minds and muscles refused to function.

Men had vanished. They had merged into a turgid mass of slowly billowing smoke and sand. Two thousand feet below the helicopter, it spread like an evil sea, or like the opening of some vile flower.

At first, the colour context was grey and brown. But abruptly it changed. It became slashed with lurid scarlet as the petrol dump ignited and rivers of flame appeared.

Still on his knees, Radford saw just ten living creatures down there. They were the five Tuaregs and their horses. The Tuaregs were safe — they were more than a mile from the explosion area. Radford saw them fighting to control their frightened animals. Then, with robes streaming, they galloped to the east.

Now it was becoming dark in the helicopter cabin. A murky, yellowish darkness. Through it, Radford staggered back to his seat. At the same time, he found his voice.

'You've got to get higher!' he shouted to Peter. Peter yelled back: 'I know it, bud! This dust can choke the carburettors.'

He opened the throttle and changed the airscrew pitch. They felt their bodies pressing down as the machine lifted fast. Lifted out of the murk and into clear air again. Pete hovered at three and a half thousand feet. Then he muttered: 'We've got to get right away from here!'

Radford gripped Peter's arm. 'No! Don't move yet . . . we stay where we are!'

The American turned a contorted face to him. 'That's crazy! There could be more rockets! One of them might hit us!'

'There's less chance of being hit if we stay high over the target. If we start moving away, we could get in the path of a missile if it's off course!'

Professor Tiere was now on his feet. He was groping for his pince-nez as he nodded agreement. '*Oui*. That's right! If we remain here, any more rockets will most likely pass under us, like . . . the one that's just exploded!'

All three of them again stared down. Now the flames were dying. Only a mist of dust was to be seen, the top of it less than five hundred feet below them. And it was continuing to spread. Already it seemed to cover an area of at least half a mile in diameter.

Radford turned to the radio in front of him. He pressed down the main switch and there was a reassuring hum from warming valves.

'This is the first job,' he said. 'I'll have to make contact with headquarters.'

He adjusted the frequency band and drew the microphone towards him. In a hoarse voice, he gave their call code.

'PKY here . . . PKY calling Sidi bel Abbes . . . '

For seconds there was no answer. Only static crackling emerged from the amplifier. Then a voice came from hundreds of miles away.

'Sidi bel Abbes to PKY . . . we are receiving you . . . transmit message.'

Radford had to gather himself before speaking again into the microphone. Had to select words which would explain clearly and briefly, yet with every important detail. It was far from easy, for he had not yet fully recovered from the first shock. And at the back of his mind was the possibility of other rockets arriving. In his first careful sentence he announced the bare fact of the new attack.

The reaction was much as he had expected.

'Please repeat that, *mon capitaine*,' the voice said from headquarters.

Radford did so. There was a short silence. Then the operator said: 'Don't continue just yet . . . wait for half a minute.'

He was a sergeant, that radio operator in the communications room at headquarters. In his time, he had received and transmitted tens of thousands of routine messages which caused no more excitement than the serving of a cup of coffee. On a few occasions he had dealt with signals of vital importance, but he could count those on the fingers of one hand. And, even though he was forbidden to discuss them except in the course of duty, they all lived in his memory because they were so unusual. Yet never, in all his experience, had he received a message quite like this which was coming from one of the helicopters.

He pressed two switches on his desk. One of them set an electronic machine in motion which automatically recorded every word spoken. The other relayed the transmission to the room occupied by the general officer commanding, so that he could not only hear the conversation, but take part in it, too, if he wished. The orders were that the last switch must only be used under circumstances of the gravest emergency. The sergeant had no qualms about his right to use it now.

'Please carry on, *mon capitaine*,' he said into his microphone after the short interval.

Radford finished his report. He took out his handkerchief and mopped his face. As he was putting it back in his pocket, a faintly familiar voice came through the amplifier — a voice he had heard at headquarters earlier that day.

'This is the G.O.C. here,' it was saying. 'I have heard your report. I take it that so far, at least, you have seen only one missile land?'

Peter mumbled under his breath: 'Doesn't he think that's enough?'

Radford managed a taut, strained grin at the American. Then he said into the microphone: 'Only one, *mon generale*.'

'And . . . and can there be . . . ?'

Radford finished the question for him and gave the answer.

'Can anyone be alive down there? No, I think it's quite impossible. But when the dust has cleared, we'll make an inspection.'

'*Non*, don't do that. If another rocket drops while you're on the ground, you also will perish. Now listen, in your report you described the missile as being guided. What makes you so sure of that?'

Professor Tiere said: 'I'll answer that.' Then, putting his lips close to the microphone, he continued: 'It was a direct hit — practically in the centre of the original crater, *mon generale*. Such accuracy would only be possible if the missile were guided in some way.'

'But what way?' Through the crackling in the ether, a note of confused impatience could be heard in the G.O.C.'s voice.

'I don't know for sure, but I think long-range radar is likely. I have already examined fragments of the first rocket, and they made me suspect — '

'You mean that somewhere in the Asben Plateau the rockets are being launched and their progress watched and guided through a radar screen? This . . . this gets yet more incredible!'

Professor Tiere made a Gallic gesture with his hands before replying. And when he did so, there was confidence in his words. For he was speaking of matters about which he knew far more than the far-distant general.

'It's not at all incredible,' he said. 'Consider the facts . . . '

Professor Tiere reminded the G.O.C. that for years it had been possible to control the flight of rockets by radar. Once the exact position of a target had been established, almost pinhead accuracy was possible at ranges of up to a thousand miles.

And somewhere amid the folds of the plateau there *must* be a rocket base. A very advanced type of base, complete with complex electronic equipment and the men to operate it. How had it been put there? And by whom? They were separate questions, but the basic fact remained.

Then the professor put forward his theory that the second missile had been launched deliberately to exterminate the experts who were examining the area. Those on the plateau — whoever they were — must be determined that expert reports should not reach French headquarters. And it must have been obvious to them that by this time many investigators would be probing the rubble.

So this last rocket had come. And it would have entirely succeeded, but for the lucky chance that the three of them had just taken off in the helicopter.

The professor finished by saying that he did not now think that another missile was likely to be launched for some time. There would be no point in sending one over at least until more scientists had had time to arrive on the scene.

As he listened to him, Radford felt an increasing admiration for the French professor. That plump little man had a brilliantly logical brain. He had courage, too, as his next words proved.

'I feel we must continue with our plan to make an immediate survey of the plateau,' he said. 'There's nothing to be gained by delay . . . '

Nothing to be gained by delay!

At his headquarters in Sidi bel Abbes, the G.O.C. repeated the professor's words to himself. He was an orthodox soldier. He had a firm grip of strategy and an excellent knowledge of modern military tactics. His record in the Second World War, when he had fought with the Free French, had shown that he could also act decisively and with imagination.

But this . . .

This was something beyond anything he had ever thought possible. For the first time in his military career, he wished that he could ask for advice before taking a decision. But there was no time to seek advice. He must decide immediately whether to let those three survivors make a survey. If they were successful and returned safely, no one would bother to congratulate him for being right. It would merely be said that he had done the obvious thing. But if they failed, if they also were lost, then he would be condemned as an irresponsible fool who had sent three valuable men to their deaths. That was one of the many burdens of high command.

He said slowly into the microphone on his walnut desk: 'Take a careful look at the plateau. Radio back reports to me every half hour. We'll have to risk their being heard by other ears. You won't have enough fuel to return here, but get as far towards Sidi bel Abbes as you can, then transmit your position, and help will be sent to you. *Bon chance, mes amis.*'

They were over the northern slopes of the Asben Plateau. Seven hundred feet below, they stared at the shelving rocks, which stretched stark and lonely into eternity. For hundreds of miles they stretched, making vast gullies of everlasting shadow, and gaunt hills where nothing grew save cacti. Occasionally, between those hills, there were flat regions of sand. But they, too, were uncanny places, for they were hemmed in by towering cliffs.

At times, they had descended to within a few feet of ground level. At others, they had risen high, to get a wide view. But always it had been the same — the only life they had seen were the cacti.

Peter was keeping an eye on his fuel gauge. He said: 'Another five minutes, then we'll have to start back. As it is, we'll have to land a couple of hundred miles short of headquarters. That means we'll have to spend a night in the Sahara before we're picked up.'

'That won't harm us,' Red said. 'We've got water and food.'

'Maybe you're right. This place sure does give me the creeps. The open desert will seem like a home from home after this.'

Professor Tiere had a chart of the area on his knee. He had been working on it with a pair of dividers and a sliding rule. Now he was drawing a cross on it. Suddenly he said: 'I'm sure we're not far from the launching area. I saw the trajectory of that rocket and the angle of the vapour trails. So, I take a bearing from the fort and the rest is not difficult — just a mathematical calculation.'

Radford, who knew exactly what the professor meant, nodded and said: 'But it leaves a fair margin for error.'

'That is so, and any such margin means that we could search for weeks without finding anything.'

'It's these gullies which make it all seem so hopeless,' Radford muttered. 'It's quite impossible to see the bottom of most of them because they're always in darkness, and they are too narrow to take the helicopter down.'

'Much too narrow, bud,' Peter said grimly. 'We could lose . . . hey, there's one of them right ahead!'

It was a ravine rather than a gully which had come into view. As they neared it, they could see that it was not only exceptionally deep, but unusually wide, too. At the centre, it seemed to measure at least two hundred feet between the sheer rock sides. It gradually tapered to a point at each end of its half-mile length.

Radford said: 'You might as well fly low over it, Peter.'

'Okay, but I'm not going too deep into it, even if it does look safe.'

Professor Tiere's forehead was creased in thought as he folded the chart. Radford noticed and asked: 'What's the new worry?'

'It's not so new, *mon ami*. As I've told you, I'm sure that radar is being used to direct the rockets. So it is possible that the same people are at this very moment using radar to track our movements.'

Radford nodded. 'I've had that in mind, too. But it's one of those chances we've just got to take.'

'I am wondering if the G.O.C. thought of it when he gave us permission to make this survey.'

'I don't think he did, Professor. You know, it's not very comfortable to think that the people who launch those missiles may be tracking this helicopter on a radar screen.'

While they were talking, Peter took the machine along the edge of the ravine until they were hovering over the southern end.

'Fly along the middle,' Radford told

him. 'Then, if we don't see anything, we'll make for the nice open desert.'

The helicopter moved slowly over the abyss, keeping level with the top of it. Radford and Professor Tiere gazed down, but semi-darkness hid the bottom from them.

Radford said: 'Can we go a little way down? We're wasting time staying at this height.'

'Not on your life,' Peter told him. 'It's not only a matter of our skins. I have to remember that this crate's United States property. I'm not taking that kind of risk.'

'There isn't so much risk — midway along there's plenty of space at each side.'

'Plenty of space where we can see. But down there where it's dark, the cliffs might close in fast and I might hit them. If that happened, we'd get to the bottom all right — the quick way. And there we'd stay.'

Radford admitted to himself that the American was probably right. But it annoyed him to have to remain at this height and gaze into thick gloom. They were halfway along the length of the ravine, and at the place where it was widest, when the professor looked at his watch.

'It's nearly time to make another report to headquarters,' he said.

'I'll wait till we've completed this examination,' Radford said. 'With all these rocks around, long-distance transmission and reception will be impossible. I have . . . '

A cough came over their radio amplifier.

A very clear cough. Such as could only be made from a transmitter which was very, very close to them.

All of them swung round to stare at the amplifier. All were blinking with astonishment.

Then they heard the voice. It was a harshly brittle voice, speaking with a heavy accent.

'Listen to me carefully,' it said. 'And obey me precisely. Your lives depend upon it.'

The voice paused, as if allowing time for the words to take effect. Radford, Professor Tiere and Peter continued to gaze at the amplifier as if hypnotised.

'You will descend immediately into the

ravine. There is no danger if you keep to the centre. You have exactly thirty seconds to begin your descent, otherwise you will be destroyed!'

Radford had a reputation for unfailing calm, for always being able to think clearly and logically. He nearly lost it now. Scores of questions tumbled through his mind. And at the same time, he wondered in a vague way whether he was suffering some ghastly mental delusion. But a glance at the professor and Peter told him that the voice was real, for they had heard it, too. He had to force himself to switch on his microphone. Another effort was needed to keep his voice steady as he asked: 'Who's speaking? Who are you?'

'You will have the answer to that very soon — if you obey my directions. Twenty seconds left.'

Radford felt thick trickles of sweat ooze down his face. He turned to Peter. 'Gain height!' he shouted. 'Get right away from here! I'll try to put out a message to headquarters!'

Peter's hand closed on the throttle ratchet. But there it remained, unmoving.

For the voice on the amplifier was saying: 'You will be blown to pieces immediately if you attempt anything so foolish. Look!'

Thin white flames were streaking upwards, directly in front of them. They formed a deathly curtain, sometimes moving a little away, sometimes getting very close to the nose of the helicopter. They were accompanied by the sound of echoing explosions.

'Tracer bullets!' Radford said. 'There must be a battery of machine guns down there!'

The fusillade ceased as suddenly as it had begun. Peter whispered through the comparative silence: 'We're almost a sitting target!'

'That is so,' the professor said. 'It's impossible for us to see them because they're in semi-darkness. But we're in full daylight up here, and they have a perfect view of us!'

'Eight seconds to go . . . seven . . . six . . . '

The harsh voice came to them through the ether, showing no trace of emotion. They had no choice about it, unless they wanted to die.

Radford said into the microphone: 'We're coming down.'

'You are wise. Keep to the centre of the ravine and you will be safe.' Peter wiped his brow with the sleeve of his tunic. Then he manoeuvred the machine into position before feathering the main prop.

Their slow descent had begun. It was like being lowered gently into a murky trap where an unknown terror awaited to pounce upon them.

4

Fatal Hour

Seen from above, the darkness had seemed all but impenetrable. But now that they were amid it, they found that this was not so. With difficulty, they could see the brooding rock walls on each side. They became more and more difficult to discern as they fell, but even after descending four hundred feet they could still be seen. Still there was no sight of the ground.

That cough came again over the amplifier.

'You have about one hundred feet to go,' it said. 'Your position is perfect. When you land, switch off the motors and immediately come out of the right-hand door.'

Peter readjusted the main prop, so that their descent became even slower. It became almost as gradual as a balloon which was only slightly underinflated.

Ahead, Radford had a dim impression of seeing what could have been the skeleton of some enormous prehistoric monster. He craned forward, but in the heavy twilight no detail could be made out.

A very slight shock jarred their seats. Then the helicopter seemed to settle and squat. They had touched ground at the bottom of the ravine. Peter hesitated for a moment before killing the main engine and the tail fan. At the same time, Radford threw up a large switch which was placed just below the roof, entirely disconnecting the radio. Now nothing that they said could be heard outside.

'Listen,' he said urgently, 'we don't know what's going to happen to us, but it's a fair bet that we've reached the rocket launching site. That means we must learn all we can as fast as we can. Then at least one of us must get the information to headquarters. I don't know how we're going to do it, but it'll have to be done.'

Professor Tiere fluttered his hands.

'*Tiens!* But all that is so obvious, Radford!'

'Perhaps it is. But it leads to something else that we've got to settle now — it could be that all of us won't be able to get away.'

There was a momentary silence. Then Peter drawled: 'You mean one or two of us might have to stay right here, just so the other can escape?'

'That's it. If it comes to the point, we may not be able to afford any heroics about all standing together. One of us must get a message to headquarters.'

Professor Tiere nodded. And Peter said: 'That sure does sound like sense to me.'

They unbolted the door and swung it open. The steel ladder was secured. Radford leading, they left the machine.

Radford had one foot on the ground when he involuntarily closed his eyes. He raised a hand to shield them as he turned round. He had been temporarily blinded by sudden and glaringly intense light. As he became used to it, he slowly reopened his eyelids. The entire ravine was illuminated by powerful floodlamps which hung from the sides of the cliffs.

Professor Tiere whispered: '*Ciel!* It's as light as the Rue de Rivoli at midnight!'

'Maybe,' Radford said. 'But they don't have rocket-launching ramps in the middle of Paris.'

As he finished speaking, he pointed. Then they all saw it — the structure which a few minutes before had seemed like a vast skeleton. It was made of steel girders, sloping up at an angle of about seventy degrees. Its highest point was fully ninety feet from the ground.

And cradled on it was a rocket.

That rocket looked as long as an airliner and wide enough at its base to hold a motorcar. The great tail fins stood out like hideous blades, each of them higher than a man. Its pointed nose was aimed to the north — the north where Fort Allengrah had once stood — where great coastal cities of Africa bustled and thrived — where, farther still, sprawled the mass of Europe.

Professor Tiere pulled in a noisy breath. 'That . . . that's an inter-continental missile!' he said.

'I guessed as much,' Radford said.

'It must be much bigger than the two which have exploded so far. That could reach Paris or London with the greatest ease! But how did it get here? It's all so incredible!'

'It's not the only one, either,' Radford said.

Some distance from the ramp, three other missiles of the same giant size were lying flat on long articulated wagons. And eight smaller rockets were standing on their bases, held secure by tubular scaffolding.

In that area, thick cables sprawled like tentacles across the ground, many of them joining at a point near the foot of the launching ramp.

Tents were pitched against the ravine sides, dozens of them. Some were almost the size of marquees. Their front flaps were open, and within them bewildering masses of what looked like electronic apparatus could be seen. Other tents were of the smaller bell type, commonly used for shelter by armies. In a recess in the cliff, several small trucks were parked.

So far, they had been looking only towards the northern end of the ravine. They turned to look the other way.

It was then that they saw a tall, gaunt figure.

He was only a few yards from them. In the intense light, every detail of him could be seen clearly. His lean face was as hard as a mottled nut. His eyes were like chips of ice. Thin and shapeless lips were parted in a humourless parody of a smile. He was wearing the uniform of a colonel of the French Foreign Legion.

'Welcome,' he said. 'You are very welcome. I can promise you an entertaining time while you live here — but I fear that you will not live for long.'

They recognised the voice. It was the one which had spoken to them over the helicopter radio.

Radford moved a little in front of the others. There was a bland insolence in his expression as he met the man's stare, and a taunting indifference about the way he spoke.

'I don't think we'll find it at all entertaining being here,' he said. 'Frankly, you don't look an entertaining type. But before we part company, you might as well answer a few questions.'

'You are not in any position to interrogate me!'

'In that case, you might find it useless to interrogate us,' Radford said smoothly. He was completely relaxed, cane under his arm, hands behind his back. It might have been a pose — probably it was — but it was a very convincing one.

'What sort of questions are you thinking of asking?'

'Why, for instance, you have established a rocket base on French territory. Why rockets have been used to murder soldiers and civilians. And why you — '

A military command rang and echoed through the ravine. It was uttered in a strange tongue.

There was a clatter of military equipment, stamping of heavy boots on the iron-hard earth. At least three dozen men appeared from behind the angle of the tents, where they must have been concealed while the helicopter descended. All were in Legion uniforms, most being dressed as ordinary legionnaires. But a few wore the chevrons of N.C.O.s, and one of them had the finer quality khaki of an officer.

That officer rapped another command, and the men formed a single file across the ravine, at the same time slinging their rifles over their shoulders. There was a crisp unison about their movements which showed that they were certainly fully trained soldiers. But the commands and their drill were not French. Their rifles, however, seemed to be French Lebels. Lebel rifles were easily recognised because of their exceptionally long barrels and tube magazines.

Suddenly Radford was startled to note that about half a dozen of them were equipped with Type B, FN automatic rifles. There could be no mistaking them. The FN, which, loaded with twenty rounds, had a large grilled piston housing on the top of the barrel, plus optical backsights. Both those features were unique to the model. Yet the FNs, which had first been produced in 1955, were issued exclusively to the North Atlantic

Treaty powers. They were a standard weapon of the free western world. One would certainly not expect to see them here, where a great western power was being threatened.

The tall, gaunt man had been watching Radford. He gave a short laugh which grated. And he said: 'You're admiring our small arms as well as our rockets. Let me assure you that you are not mistaken — the rifles are genuine Lebels and the automatics are the latest FNs. But don't bother about that for the moment. I'll give a full explanation very soon. First I think we had better introduce ourselves. My name is Balazki — Colonel Balazki.'

Radford raised one eyebrow. 'You give yourself airs. You're not a colonel.'

'Not a colonel of the Legion. But I hold the rank in another and a greater army. For all of us here, this is merely a uniform of convenience. Now you will let me know exactly who and what you are!'

'Suppose we refuse?' Radford asked, curious to see what the reaction would be.

'If you are difficult, you will suffer pain

before you die. The choice is yours. We can easily establish your identities since you must be carrying personal papers.'

Radford shrugged. He said: 'My name's Hugh Radford. As you can see, I'm a captain of the Legion.'

'And your two companions?'

Radford gave their names and accurate particulars. There was nothing to be gained by not doing so. When he had finished, Balazki's iced eyes narrowed. He looked carefully at Peter's U.S. uniform, then at the American markings on the helicopter.

'The French are indeed very afraid,' he said. 'They are independently minded people. They must be in a panic, or why else would they scurry to the Americans for help!'

For Professor Tiere that was an intolerable taunt against his country. Colour rushed into his plump face.

'You do not know us very well, monsieur! France fears nothing!'

'If you do not fear these,' he said, jerking an arrogant head towards the rockets, 'you must be as brainless as old sheep! Those missiles mean the beginning of the end for all the decadent democracies of the west, Professor! In time, they will lead to your extermination!'

The harsh voice spoke with a flat certainty, as though there could be no possible room for doubt. Then Balazki went on: 'None of you will leave this place alive, so you might just as well know all the facts. After all, that's what you came here to find out, isn't it? For myself, I'll find it most interesting to watch your reactions while I explain it all to you. But first, you will be searched and disarmed. Then you will join me in my tent . . . '

They were in that tent.

Dusk had fallen, and that usually brought sudden cold in the Sahara. But here the confined space was warmed by a powerful battery-operated strip lamp, around which clouds of flies darted and buzzed.

They sat on camp stools, Balazki opposite them and behind a trestle table which served as a desk. On the table were wire trays containing neat piles of typed memoranda, rolled charts of North Africa and the Mediterranean coast of Europe, inkwells and pens, and a box of small black cigars. Outside, two of the fraudulent legionnaires stood guard.

Balazki lit one of the cigars. He was relaxed and self-assured. 'You'll have guessed,' he said, 'that I'm a soldier of the East European powers. I belong to a group of nations which intend to finish forever the influence of France, Britain and America.'

'You've been intending that for a long time,' Radford said. 'But we're still here. Free nations aren't easily defeated or frightened.'

Balazki waved an impatient hand. 'But wait! You will not talk so glibly when I tell you about our master project. It's a plan which we'll be putting into operation in just a few hours.'

He paused. Professor Tiere said: 'Please go on, monsieur. You have us fascinated.'

'I'm glad,' Balazki said dryly. 'You'll be even more fascinated to hear that tonight rockets with nuclear warheads will be launched from this ravine. They will explode on certain carefully selected cities on the North African coast. They will be so guided that they will land on the native quarters.'

Radford asked softly: 'Are you serious?'

'I've never been more serious. The native peoples will suffer enormously in dead and injured. And naturally they will believe that the French are responsible, since the missiles will have been seen travelling from the Sahara region. You can imagine what will happen then, can't you? There will certainly be a massive native uprising against the white population of North Africa. There will be massacre, gentlemen. And in the end, the Western powers will be thrown out of this continent.'

There was another pause. Only the buzz of the flies could be heard. Then Radford said: 'You talk like a madman.'

'But I do not act like one, Captain Radford. You have already seen for yourself our missiles and the launching ramp. You have also seen what happened to the wretched Fort Allengrah. So don't insult me by speaking of madness!'

Radford nodded reluctantly. The known facts had to be faced, but many questions remained unanswered.

65

'Very well,' he said. 'But we'll understand better what you're talking about if you begin at the beginning.'

Balazki glanced at his watch. 'I haven't much time to spare, but I'll gladly give you the outline. You know, of course, that we have been trying for years to get the French out of Algeria?'

'Yes — and you stirred up a rebellion. It failed because France acted quickly,' Radford said.

'That's true. So we had to think of new ways of ending Western influence in North Africa — something original and daring was needed. We had our first germ of an idea when the French government announced that they were to test atomic weapons in the Sahara Desert.'

Professor Tiere blinked through his spectacles. 'We are entitled to test atomic devices in the same way as any other country,' he said. 'How could that give you an idea?'

'It was because of the way the Arabs took the news. Many of them were afraid. They said that atomic tests in the Sahara were dangerous. Something might go wrong, then they would suffer.'

'That's true,' Professor Tiere snapped back. 'But there was no need for the Arabs to be afraid. Our scientists are not fools — we take every precaution. We told them that. If they didn't believe us, it's only because of the lying propaganda that your nations have pumped into them!'

'Yes, we certainly encouraged them to believe in the danger,' Balazki admitted. 'At the same time, we wondered whether we could make the French tests *seem* to go wrong. Just suppose many thousands of natives were killed in nuclear explosions — *and it looked as if the French were to blame because of their Sahara tests*. What then, Professor?'

Tiere fiddled with his shirt buttons. 'It would be horrible . . . horrible beyond all description!' he muttered.

'Exactly. And there would be such fury among the native peoples that the Western nations would be swept out of North Africa like chaff. Now can you imagine the next problem we had to solve?'

'I think I can,' Radford said. 'But you tell us.'

'We had to find a way of launching atomic missiles on the natives *from the Sahara*, so that the whole world would believe they were French. We have found a way. Everything is here in this ravine — waiting to be fired.'

Radford said slowly: 'You must have brought everything here by air — the equipment, the scientists and soldiers.'

'We did — but you move too fast, Captain Radford. First we had to make the most careful aerial surveys of the Sahara. There, the sheer size of French North Africa helped us. It's so easy for planes, flying at high altitudes, to penetrate far into the desert without being seen. True, there are radar stations on the coast, but they are all located near the big ports. It's only necessary to keep well away from those areas. Our first move was to investigate this Asben Plateau region. Our aircraft took hundreds of photographs of it before we decided that this ravine and its surroundings were perfect for our purpose. Infrared pictures, which cut through darkness, showed all the details. We even spotted a natural water supply. And we noted that the rock sides were almost vertical — except for a place at the south end. We saw that there a small landslide had formed rough steps leading to the bottom. We were satisfied.'

'Just a moment,' Radford said. 'You must have needed a landing ground. There are thousands of tons of equipment here. You couldn't have dropped it all by parachute.'

'We have a landing ground — a very good one.'

'Where? Don't tell me you made it!'

'No — that would have been impossible. There's a stretch of rock tableland about a mile west of here. It's almost perfectly flat and long enough to take the largest aircraft. In fact, nature also provided us with a ready-made airstrip. That was one of the points which decided us to go ahead and establish a rocket base here.'

Radford fumbled for a cigarette. Professor Tiere sat hunched forward, gazing at his feet. Peter was examining the tips of his fingers.

'You all seem a little disturbed,' Balazki added. 'But surely you must have some questions?'

'Tell us about the soldiers you have here,' Radford said. 'They're in Legion uniform. Why?'

'An interesting point,' Balazki said almost agreeably. 'First, let me tell you that all of them are carefully picked and specially trained men. They were brought here for general work and defence. It was decided to dress them like legionnaires in case they ever had to leave the ravine area — then, if they chanced to be seen, their presence would seem quite natural. I'm wearing this uniform for the same reason. As it happened, we did have to leave this ravine on one occasion. It was a very important occasion, and the fact that we looked like legionnaires proved most helpful.'

Radford suddenly gazed hard at Balazki. 'Would that have anything to do with the Arab village of Gacruss?' he asked.

'It would. Do you want to know why we went there?'

'I do.'

'It's simple enough. During our preparations, we found that a great deal of extra labour was needed to widen part of the

70

ravine. We could have flown more men out from East Europe, but that would have caused serious delays. I decided that the solution was to find a small, isolated Arab village and bring the whole population here to do the work for us. Gacruss was just right. I knew it was seldom visited by anyone and was only two days' march from here. So we went there for our slave labour. The operation was quite successful — except for one small thing.' Balazki paused, looking thoughtful.

Radford said: 'The small thing would be the fact that you did not kill the old headman — an Arab named Taiba.'

Balazki nodded. 'Right again. I thought he'd die anyway. I was surprised when our radio listening post picked up signals revealing that he had reached Fort Allengrah.'

'Was that why you used rockets to destroy the fort?'

'No. Our preparations were well advanced and we judged ourselves quite safe from discovery and counteraction.'

'Then why did you destroy it?' asked Radford.

'Merely to test our missile guiding

system. Remember that all our rockets and electronic equipment were flown here in separate parts and assembled in the ravine. We had to be sure of absolute accuracy. The only way to be certain of that was to fire at a medium-distance target and see what happened. Fort Allengrah was just right. Its sudden radio silence told us that we had made direct hits, and that was confirmed by messages we picked up from Sidi bel Abbes.'

Professor Tiere said with incredulous horror: 'So you slaughtered the whole garrison just . . . just as a test of missile accuracy!'

'It was a very important test, I assure you. So the garrison didn't die for nothing, did they?' He gave a short laugh and added: 'Of course, we did not waste valuable nuclear warheads on them. Conventional explosives were enough.'

Radford asked: 'Why the second attack — the one on the men who were examining the ruins?'

'There was nothing — er — nothing personal about it. We'd made some minor adjustments and needed one further test.

Again, we knew that your own radio signals would tell of our success. You three in the helicopter were very lucky to escape. I listened with great interest to your talk with the G.O.C. at Sidi bel Abbes after the explosion and decided that even if you did find the ravine you could do us no harm, since you could be forced into it before being able to use your radio.'

Radford stubbed out his cigarette. Now the whole hideous pattern was taking shape. It was so monstrous that he had to struggle to keep his brain clear. Then a sudden thought occurred to him.

'Those Arabs you abducted from Gacruss,' he said. 'Where are they?'

'Camped at their usual place at the south end of the ravine. They're exhausted, for we've driven them hard, but most have survived.'

'What will you do with them?'

Balazki shrugged. 'They can go free when the missiles have been fired. They can do us no harm then — not with all North Africa aflame. Who would listen to them? We'll leave them to find their own way out of the ravine — up the pathway I mentioned. It's a fairly easy route, except for one place where we've fixed a rope ladder, a — '

Radford cut in: 'Your soldiers are armed with Lebels and FN automatic rifles. Any particular reason?'

'Just to add conviction to their role as Western soldiers — and perhaps to cause confusion. It's attention to details such as that which is important, Captain Radford.'

Radford took off his *kepi* and dabbed sweat from his forehead. The rest was perfectly clear. Those rumours of huge 'guns' being erected on the plateau must have been started by some passing tribesmen who saw the rockets being lowered into the ravine. And the Arabs who claimed to have been chased by 'giant birds of prey' had certainly seen the great transport planes approaching the airstrip.

'You are impressed?' Colonel Balazki asked. He was leaning back behind his trestle table and lighting another small cigar.

Radford said: 'I'd never have imagined that human beings could plan anything so ghastly.'

'Ghastly? Well, yes I suppose it is. But it serves a great purpose, for it will lead to the utter destruction of your Western democracies. To achieve that, all methods are justified.'

'Have you thought of the cost in lives — of the utter horror when your nuclear missiles explode?'

'Naturally, but it doesn't worry me at all. You people of the West have been made soft by sentiment. We cannot allow such luxuries to interfere with plans for world mastery.'

'Have your targets been settled?' Radford asked.

'They have. We have been ordered to fire nuclear missiles on the native quarters of Casablanca, Oran, Algiers and Tunis!'

All three of them drew in a swift, horrified breath.

Casablanca, in Morocco, was one of the world's great ports. Although Morocco had been granted independence, the country remained an important sphere of Western influence and many white people lived there.

Oran, with its superb harbour, was a

vital N.A.T.O. naval base in Algeria. And Algiers, the seething capital of the dependency, had a quarter of a million Arabs living in its vast maze of narrow, fetid streets.

Tunis was the site of an ancient Arab city — a place of beautiful mosques and of great religious importance to the people of Islam.

Radford could imagine it all happening. In his mind's eye, he could see the missiles descending. Their trails left by sodium flares would suggest that they had been fired by the French from the Sahara. He could imagine the awful havoc as the atomic warheads exploded in the packed native quarters of the four cities.

Then would come the blood-lusting fury of millions of Arabs. They would scream that, in spite of their protests, the French had insisted on the nuclear tests. They would say: 'Now see what has happened! Those tests have not only gone wrong, but whole Arab populations have died horribly as a result! But white people have not suffered! The cursed Europeans have looked after their own kind!'

The fury of the native peoples would certainly drive every white settler and soldier out of North Africa. But only after many had been slaughtered in anti-Western riots.

Soon after that, the European dictators would take control of North Africa and threaten the democracies. The whole cause of freedom would suffer a crippling blow.

The prospect almost made Radford's brain reel. He braced himself before asking the final question.

'When exactly are you to make the attacks?'

Balazki gave a thin smile. He looked at his watch.

'In just five hours,' he said. 'The first nuclear missile will be launched towards Casablanca at ten o'clock tonight. The three other cities will be attacked at twelve-minute intervals. At thirty-six minutes past ten, the whole operation will be complete!'

5

Emergency Action

Catastrophe in five hours ... A mere three hundred minutes to go, then an outrage which would shatter and darken the free world. It was as unavoidable as the setting of the sun — unless somehow, something could be done to prevent those hideous atomic devices being launched.

But what?

The cause of all humanity lay with three prisoners in a remote Sahara ravine. A ravine which was filled with highly trained and well-armed enemy soldiers. It was absurd even to imagine that they could get anywhere near the missiles.

Could a message be radioed to Sidi bel Abbes, giving the awful facts and the location of the ravine? If that could be done within the next hour, there might just be time for French heavy bombers to blast the place to dust. But what hope was there of being able to send such a message? Absolutely none. It would first be necessary to seize the ravine's radio equipment. Red knew that a battalion of Britain's Brigade of Guards would have their work cut out to do that. To think that he, with Peter and the elderly Professor Tiere, could do so, was just another flight of fancy.

What about the helicopter? That did not seem to offer any chance, either. A miracle would be needed to reach it alive. Then, so that its radio could be used, it would have to be flown high above the peaks and kept there for several minutes. To achieve that would require yet another miracle, for they would be an easy target for the machine guns.

But just suppose they did succeed in flashing an SOS to Sidi bel Abbes? What would Balazki do then? To Radford, the answer was obvious — Balazki would not wait for the French planes to arrive. He would forget about the planned timetable and launch his rockets immediately. So the only result would be that disaster would strike just that little bit sooner.

Everything pointed to the fact that they were as helpless as trussed chickens. That with all humanity on the edge of indescribable terror, all they could do was wait and watch.

Radford felt a pulse thudding deep in his brain. It seemed to be saying: 'Try anything . . . try anything . . .

And he thought: *I would try anything! But there's nothing to try!*

For the first time in his long experience as a special agent, Hugh Radford was near the point of utter defeat. Balazki must have known that, for he said: 'What cannot be avoided might as well be accepted, Captain Radford. The short time you and your friends have to live can be spent in an interesting way, if you behave yourselves. I'm sure you will be fascinated by the firing of our missiles. Many new devices are being used by our Dr. Goerler to meet the special problems of . . . ah! But here's the man himself.'

The tent flaps had parted. A tiny furrowed face peeped cautiously in, like that of an old and slightly mischievous elf. At first sight, there was something almost pleasing about it. Until one noticed the eyes. Heavily bloodshot eyes, they were. Not oval, either, but as round as those of a young hog. In their own way, they were as hard as those of Balazki. But the stark lights of twisted genius showed there, too. No one willingly met Dr. Goerler's gaze.

'May I come in?' Dr. Goerler asked in a high piping voice, still only his head showing.

'But certainly, Doctor,' Balazki said. 'You must be curious to meet our new arrivals.'

'Oh, but I am indeed,' Goerler piped. Leaning on his stick, he limped into the tent. He stopped to stare at Radford, Peter and Professor Tiere. It was the French scientist who interested him most.

'I've heard much about you, Professor,' Goerler went on. 'In your own field you have done interesting work — very interesting. I did not expect to meet a western nuclear physicist during my stay in this ravine. I wish you'd arrived earlier, for we could have had useful talks, couldn't we? But as it is, there's so little time.'

'*Monsieur le docteur,* so far as I am

concerned there's no time at all,' Tiere said dryly. 'I have not been introduced to you, and I do not want to be introduced!'

Goerler did not seem worried by the rebuff. 'You must be reasonable,' he said in his high-pitched tones. 'We men of science have so much in common that — '

'You and I have nothing in common!' Professor Tiere snapped back. 'Science should aid humanity! You work only for its destruction!'

Radford was only partly listening to the exchange. His brain was working at the speed of light. The arrival of Dr. Goerler had introduced a new situation. On the face of it, only a trivial situation. But trivialities could be exploited. Sometimes they could be used to bring about a surprise advantage. Perhaps he could bring just that about now. Perhaps . . .

'Professor — I think you're going too far,' Radford said slowly and thoughtfully.

All of them showed various degrees of astonishment. But the most shaken was Tiere himself.

'Too far!' Tiere repeated after taking several seconds to recover. Then he added firmly: 'Hugh, it cannot be that you expect me to talk in a friendly way with this — '

'I don't see why not,' Radford interrupted.

Tiere threw out his arms. 'But he will help to kill tens of thousands of helpless people! Some have already died! We are to die, too! The man is a monster among many other monsters! Radford, you cannot be serious! Not you, a Briton and a captain of the *legion etrangere* — '

'I know how you feel, but I think we ought to be realistic,' Radford said, looking around him. 'We have lost. Balazki, Goerler and their friends have won, and there's nothing we can do to alter that. So what's to be gained by snarling at each other? I for one would much rather spend my last few hours on earth pleasantly — wouldn't you, Peter?'

He finished by staring hard at the American. Peter was nobody's fool. And, being an air pilot, he was used to thinking fast. He could not guess what Radford was getting at, but he knew instinctively that Radford had some idea at the back of his mind and was seeking support. Peter gave it. He nodded emphatically.

'I couldn't agree with you more,' he said. 'Let's all at least try to be buddies.'

Radford stood up. He said to Balazki: 'Professor Tiere does not want to be civil to Dr. Goerler, but I do. The way I see it, all of us here have just been doing our duty and we've been unlucky. I don't like what you're going to do — but then no man ever liked what his enemies were going to do, so there's nothing unusual about that. I'd . . . ' Radford hesitated, then added diffidently, 'I'd like to give a lead to my friend Tiere by shaking Dr. Goerler by the hand.'

'This is indeed an extraordinary change,' Balazki said, watching Red carefully.

'Not really. Like you, I'm a soldier. We soldiers fight as long as there's a chance of victory. But only lunatics go on resisting when all hope has gone. That's true, isn't it?'

'Very true, Captain Radford. I admire your common sense. You have shown a logical side to your character which comes as a pleasant surprise to me. There is a lot of information you can give us, and now we can hear it in a friendly way.'

Radford smiled. With arm partly outstretched, he moved across the front of the trestle table towards Goerler. After a momentary hesitation, Peter got off his chair and followed Radford, keeping slightly to one side of him. The American was acting on a strong hunch that this was what Radford wanted him to do. Balazki leaned forward, satisfied amusement on his lean and mottled face.

Radford said to Goerler: 'Here's two of us who don't mind shaking your hand. Whatever Professor Tiere may think, there can — '

Then it happened. The easy flow of words suddenly stopped, as if cut off by a switch. And in the same fraction of a second Radford was moving with deadly, almost incredible speed.

His extended right hand streaked outwards, his body pivoting with it. The hand was open. And it was perfectly flat. It moved like a butcher's cleaver. The outer edge of the hand whipped into the side of Balazki's neck.

It was a paralysing blow. An attack move which was familiar to all experts in close combat. And Radford was very expert. The effect was immediate. The main nerve channels linking Balazki's brain and body became temporarily numb. His jaw fell slack and his eyes rolled till only the whites showed. He gave a faint gasp as he slumped forward over the table. Then he began to slide towards the floor. But Radford caught him beneath the shoulders and controlled the fall, so that no noise was made which might attract the guards outside.

At the same time, Radford whispered: 'Peter — see to Goerler!'

But there was no need for the order. Peter had acted almost as fast as Radford. Pouncing on Goerler from behind, he pressed a hand hard over the doctor's mouth. Goerler wriggled, but he could do no more in the American's immensely strong grip. He tried to wave his stick, but with his free hand Peter snatched it away from him.

Meantime, Radford was kneeling beside the still unconscious Balazki. He was unfastening the two press-studs which secured the top of the colonel's pistol holster. From out of it he pulled a 7.92 mm. Borchardt-Luger. The weight of the weapon immediately told him that it was fully loaded with eight rounds in the butt magazine. But as with all army pistols and revolvers, a length of strong cord was knotted to a ring at the heel of the butt. The other end of the cord was secured to the Sam Browne belt. It was a simple device to prevent the pistol being dropped. That cord had to be parted.

Professor Tiere saw to that. He was now recovering his wits and he knelt beside Red, producing a small pocket knife. With it, he cut the gun free.

Radford stood up, at the same time cocking the Luger so as to bring a cartridge out of the magazine and into the barrel.

Peter asked quietly: 'Where do we go from here?'

'I hope we'll go a long way. But first we've got to wait for Balazki to wake up. We need him because — '

He broke off and sniffed. Then Peter and Professor Tiere sniffed, too. There was an acrid tang in the air. It was smoke.

87

Flames were coming from a well-filled wastepaper basket which was near the table. A draught was bending them towards the tent canvas.

Peter said: 'Get it out quick, or we'll be in the middle of a furnace!'

Balazki's cigar must have caused the blaze by rolling into the basket when he was knocked out.

Radford plunged a foot into the middle of the fire, his leather leggings protecting him from burns. He stamped as hard as he dared — but that was not too hard, for any unusual noise might attract the sentries. There was also the danger that the smoke might become thick enough to billow out and be seen. There was a tense minute while Radford used his boot. But at the end of that time he had extinguished the fire. It had left a thin smoke haze which was quickly dispersing. That crisis had been averted, but it had been a very close call.

Now Radford noticed that Balazki was stirring. He twitched as he lay on the ground. Then he shook his head and instinctively put a hand to his neck. His eyes flickered open. They blinked dazedly, then sprang into focus. They were looking into the viciously efficient barrel of the Luger. Radford was bending over him and holding the pistol only six inches from his face.

'If you call for help, if you make any noise at all, I'll kill you,' Radford told him. He was whispering. But there was stinging emphasis in every word. They had the impact of drops of acid. Balazki knew — all of them knew — that Radford would do just that. If necessary, he would kill.

Balazki was tough and he was no coward. But at this moment he could not argue, could not resist. He gave a slow nod.

Radford turned towards Dr. Goerler. The scientist was shaking in Peter's grip as if a series of high-voltage shocks were being put through his body. Terror showed in his round, pink eyes. There was not likely to be any resistance from him.

'The same applies to you,' Radford told Goerler. 'If you want to go on living, keep quiet and keep still!'

At a sign from Radford, Peter took his hand from over Goerler's mouth. For a second, it seemed as if the quivering fellow would collapse. But he managed to sway onto a stool.

Radford turned again to Balazki. 'Get to your feet,' he said curtly. Balazki obeyed. He was breathing quickly, but already he was recovering from the worst effects of the neck blow.

'Listen to me carefully.' Radford continued. 'And that means you, too, Goerler. We're going to walk out of this tent — all five of us. We'll move towards the helicopter. It will look as if it's your idea, Balazki. You will persuade the guards that everything's in order — and you'll remember that if anything goes wrong, I'll be right behind you with this gun in my pocket and I'll use it to kill you first, then Goerler. We'll all get into the helicopter. We'll take off, and after — '

Balazki interrupted, 'The strain must be driving you mad, Captain Radford. I have soldiers posted near the helicopter. Do you really think they'll allow it to be flown away with you in it?'

'You're in command here, aren't you?'

'I am, but — '

'They'll obey you. It will be your job to make it seem convincing. You will tell them that there are some interesting devices in the machine which you and the doctor want to see operating in flight. Say that we will rise only to the top of the ravine, stay there for a few minutes, then descend.'

Balazki gazed hard at Radford. 'It looks as if you're serious.'

'I've never been more serious.'

'But you can't imagine that we can all get into the machine and take off without arousing suspicion. And even if you do succeed in that, what can you gain? If you're thinking of transmitting a message to Sidi bel Abbes, let me remind you that it would be heard on our monitoring system. Suppose you managed to radio the facts and give the position of this ravine — what then? It would serve no purpose. There would be only one result — the rockets would be fired immediately. They would explode on their targets long before the French could do anything to interfere.'

Radford nodded. 'I have thought of that, Balazki.'

'Then what have you got in mind?'

'That need not concern you. Anyway, not just yet. All you have to do is to see that we all get into the helicopter and take off without interference. You'll die if we don't.'

Balazki braced himself. He said slowly: 'Suppose I choose to die now? Suppose I challenge you to pull that trigger?'

'Then I *shall* pull it. You have told us that we are to die in any case, so we've nothing to lose. You have three seconds to make up your mind. If you want me to kill you now, I'll oblige. Then I'll also put a bullet into Goerler. In a way, it might be the best thing. The world would be a cleaner place without the two of you!'

Goerler produced a stifled whine. He looked pleadingly from his stool at Balazki.

'He means it! Don't let him . . . you mustn't let him kill me! I'm a valuable scientist . . . '

Radford said: 'I'm starting to count now. Remember, after three seconds I use this gun. *One . . . two . . . '* Balazki parted his lips into a blending of a smile and a snarl.

'Very well — I see no reason to sacrifice my life uselessly since your scheme, whatever it may be, is bound to come to nothing.'

'You're being sensible now. Remember that this must look convincing. If it doesn't, your life will still be sacrificed. You will leave this tent first, with Peter and Professor Tiere at each side of you. Make any excuse you like to the sentries if you think one is necessary. I'll be following just a pace behind, with Dr. Goerler.'

Balazki shrugged. He looked as if he might make another protest. But finally he moved towards the tent flap. Peter and Professor Tiere fell into step beside him. Radford put the Luger into his right-hand tunic pocket, keeping his fingers round the heavy butt. He jerked his head at Goerler, who made an effort to get to his feet, but flopped back onto the stool. It seemed that the scientist's shaking frame was incapable of supporting him.

'You'll have to do better than that,' Radford said. 'Just remember what'll happen to you if anything goes wrong.'

Goerler made another attempt. This time he was more successful. Radford pushed him after the others.

'Start talking to me,' he ordered. 'Start boasting about those rockets of yours.'

Goerler talked. He did so in tones which reached a full octave above their high-pitched norm, so that he almost trilled. And he quoted technical specifications which were meaningless to Radford. But they served the purpose of partly disguising his true state of terror.

They followed Balazki, Peter and Professor Tiere out of the tent.

There, the two sentries were slapping their rifle butts in a salute, which Balazki returned by raising his cane. They moved across the starkly illuminated ravine towards the helicopter, which was about a hundred yards away. Another couple of soldiers were guarding the machine, standing *a repos* on each side of it. In their Legion uniforms, it was almost impossible to believe that they were not friendly. At first glance, at least, they looked typical legionnaires.

Other soldiers — all of them apparently off duty — could be seen sprawling on the ground towards the north end of the ravine, where brooded the great mass of the missile launching ramp. In the marquees, men in civilian clothes were seated before panels of electronic instruments, or talking in small groups. At the far southern end it was possible to see a huddle of people, most of them sitting on their haunches, and a few soldiers guarding them. They were the captive Arabs.

Over the whole place there was an atmosphere of tension. Of waiting anxiously for the time to come when all the work of recent weeks would reach its climax. The moment when the rockets would rise miles above the earth, then turn to the far-off coastal cities. But Radford was concentrating on Balazki, who was walking a pace ahead of him, and on the helicopter guards. They were less than fifty yards away now. They had seen Balazki and were shouldering their Lebels for a salute.

Radford spoke without moving his lips. He said: 'Remember to sound convincing . . . your life and Goerler's depend on it!'

The sentries saluted. Again Balazki raised his cane. The helicopter's door was open and the steel steps were hanging from it. The group of five stopped when only a few feet from those steps.

Balazki said to the nearest of the soldiers: 'I am going to — '

A shout interrupted him. An officer was striding towards them. He was wearing the badges of a major. Radford recognised him as the one they had seen on first landing.

Radford whispered to Balazki: 'It looks as if your aide is going to ask questions. I'm relying on you to answer them. I've still got my hand round the Luger!'

As he got closer, the major broke into a trot. When he reached them, he looked cautiously at Balazki.

'Is everything all right?' he asked.

Radford moved very slightly, so that the muzzle of his concealed gun pressed lightly against the base of Balazki's spine.

'Quite all right,' Balazki said.

'But I don't understand . . . what are you doing?'

Radford increased the gun pressure on Balazki's spine. 'It's perfectly simple. Our guests have been telling me about this helicopter. It seems it carries some . . . some rather unusual devices which Dr. Goerler is anxious to test.'

The major seemed partly satisfied. 'In that case, perhaps we'd better increase the guard while Dr. Goerler is making his inspection.'

'There's no point in doing that. We'll be taking the machine off the ground.'

Astonishment came to the major's face. 'Surely you can't mean that you and Dr. Goerler are going to fly with the three prisoners! It seems most undesirable, even dangerous.'

Balazki was uncomfortably conscious of the gun in his back. And of the cold determination of the man who was holding it. He was also confident that nothing could be done to upset the rocket-firing plans. So he continued his effort to sound plausible.

'It appears that we have to take the helicopter up because it's the only way the devices can be demonstrated,' he said. 'We'll simply rise to the top of the ravine, stay there a few minutes, then come down again.'

'But Colonel — why take the prisoners with you? We have several men here who can fly a helicopter such as this. It seems to be a perfectly standard American type.'

'Things are not always what they seem. I am satisfied that the presence of all three prisoners is necessary to show us how the devices work.'

The major looked at each of the group in turn, his eyes resting particularly on Goerler. 'Are you all right, Doctor?' he asked.

'Yes . . . yes, I'm quite all right,' Goerler answered, nodding vigorously.

'You look a little ill.'

'He's not ill,' Balazki said, as Radford gave a slight twist to the gun. 'Just a little tense, I think, as our zero hour approaches.'

The major turned again to Balazki. 'I ask you to think of the risk if you fly in that machine with these men. You and Goerler will be outnumbered and alone.'

Balazki shrugged. 'But what can they do? After all, I am armed and they are not.'

There was a pause. A very long pause. It ended when the major said heavily:

'You say you are armed, Colonel?'

And as he spoke his eyes were fixed on Balazki's holster.

On Balazki's empty holster. And on a length of cut cord which hung from the Sam Browne belt.

6

The Crash

Radford followed the direction of the major's gaze.

He was a fraction of a second ahead of the others in understanding what had happened. Just a fraction. But even in such a tiny fragment of time, a highly trained mind can assess all the facts of a new emergency, reach a decision and act on it. Radford did exactly that.

He knew there was no chance now of getting into the helicopter and taking off without causing alarm. Even if he could use the Luger to force Balazki and the major into the machine, the two guards were still there. They would interfere drastically.

But there was one slender advantage for Radford, Peter and Professor Tiere — they were within a few feet of the helicopter. They might be able to get into it. Might be able to hold the others back while they took off. Might . . .

As realisation was dawning on the others, Radford's gun came out of his tunic pocket. With his free hand, he gave Balazki a vicious push. Balazki, taken by surprise, staggered forward against the major. The major was reaching for his own pistol, but the impact of Balazki's body knocked his arm down before he could grip the butt.

At the same time, Radford shouted: 'Peter! Professor! Get in the 'copter! Start the motors!'

The two sentries were moving. Like all the other soldiers, they were not only exceptionally tough, they had also been picked for their intelligence. They had heard the exchanges between Balazki and the major. They understood what was happening and they reacted immediately.

They did not make the mistake of rushing forward to prevent Peter and the professor entering the helicopter. Had they done that, their long rifles would have been a hindrance, since they were not designed for close-quarter combat.

Instead, the two men stood back, bringing their Lebels up to their shoulders. Each was bringing his sights to bear on Radford.

★　★　★

But they could not fire immediately. A further couple of seconds were needed for them to release the safety catches and cock the rifles by jerking the bolts back, then forward.

In that time, Radford used his Luger.

Accurate aim was out of the question. He had to act too fast for that. And he was not yet familiar with this particular pistol. Lugers as a whole, he knew well enough. But even guns of exactly the same type vary in their shooting characteristics. A man must get used to a gun before he can be sure of absolute accuracy. So Radford had to rely on some luck. He had it.

The two soldiers were close together, one just a little ahead of the other. Whirling round on one heel, Radford fired at the nearest. There was a crash which reverberated through the ravine. The spinning snub-nosed bullet hit the breech-block of the soldier's Lebel, twisting the weapon out of the man's hands. But the slug had not spent itself yet. Diverted from its course, it buried itself into the left shoulder of the other sentry. He dropped his rifle, clutching at the wound. His groan mingled with the echo of the explosion.

Meantime, the Luger's toggle-joint had doubled up like a bent thumb as, in one complete action, the empty cartridge case was ejected from the top of the barrel and a fresh round forced into position.

Radford glanced towards the helicopter. Peter was already inside it and Professor Tiere was halfway up the ladder.

A new explosion crashed through the ravine. Radford felt a brush of hot air against his cheek, as though a wasp had sped past. A clean hole appeared in the side of the helicopter a few inches below the windows.

The bullet had been fired by the major. He was crouching on one knee. His finger was tightening over the curved trigger for a second shot. The range was very close. So close that he could scarcely miss again, particularly since his pistol was sighted and held steady. Radford's gun was not sighted. He knew that he would not have time to aim it . . .

There was only one possibility. Radford took it. He kicked at the loose sand at his feet. A spray of the pellets cascaded towards the major. And, because the major was kneeling, they went directly into his face and eyes. They did so as he was squeezing the trigger.

Temporarily blinded, he jerked the gun up. The slug whistled high over Radford's head.

But Balazki had suddenly reappeared. In the last few seconds, he had moved to one side and had been pressed against the side of the helicopter. Now, hands outstretched like claws, he flung himself at Radford.

Radford sensed the attack rather than saw it. He tried to twist away from it, but only partly succeeded. One of Balazki's fingers gripped a lapel of his tunic. Off balance, both men reeled against the steel steps. Balazki's gaunt body had the strength of whipcord. And he was driven by seething fury. His *kepi* had fallen to the ground. Now he lowered his bare cropped head and butted it like a battering ram into the pit of Radford's stomach. He just had time to brace his stomach muscles against the worst effects of the blow. But even so, he felt a hot surge of pure pain as the breath was forced out of him. Then a feeling of nausea.

Balazki's head was still lowered. He was about to butt again. This time, Radford knew that he would certainly be crushed to the ground. He tried to move away, but his legs would not obey his brain.

Something crashed onto Balazki's right shoulder. Something short and formidable. And Balazki folded like a clasp knife, then lay huddled at Radford's feet.

Radford turned. He saw Tiere. The professor was leaning out of the helicopter and he was holding a heavy spanner.

'Get in!' Tiere gasped, putting out a hand to help Radford. Then he managed to add triumphantly: 'It was a good blow I gave him, *oui*?'

Radford staggered up the ladder. He fell into the helicopter, still holding the Luger.

At that moment the whole machine quivered, as if dancing on a bed of coiled springs. A roar of concentrated noise burst into their ears. Peter had started the motors. But the helicopter was not lifting.

'Get her off the ground!' Radford shouted.

'Daren't risk it — not for another minute!' Peter yelled back from the pilot's seat. 'The motors are cold. Got to let 'em warm up, or we'll stall!'

Another full minute before they could even begin to rise! To Radford, this seemed the absolute finish. His plan would be certain to come to nothing save disaster.

A fresh sound mingled with that of the motors. It was a high-pitched whine which came from one of the tents. Radford recognised it. Sweat dripping from his face, he lurched towards Peter.

'That's the general alarm,' he shouted. 'They'll have their machine guns on us in a few seconds. Try taking off now!'

'Don't talk crazy! I know these kites! We'll be sure to crash!'

'*I want you to crash! It's the only way, Peter!*'

He roared the words into Peter's ear. Peter blinked at him.

'Want me to . . . ? You gone crazy?'

'No! Get high above the launching ramp, then cut out the motors so we drop on top of it! That's the only way to stop the rockets!'

'Yeah, it'll stop the rockets, but it'll stop us too! We'll all be killed!'

'We're just three lives! If those missiles are launched, tens of thousands will die! It's worth it, isn't it?'

The American nodded. 'I figure it is, but I never counted on finishing up this way! Okay, I guess we can make it!'

He engaged the main air screw and opened the throttle. The helicopter quivered even more violently, then seemed to sway as if on the end of a swinging rope. They were airborne. Moving up vertically.

Radford turned to Tiere, who was standing close to him. 'You heard what I told Peter?'

'I did,' the professor answered.

'That was my plan all along, but I

couldn't tell you, or Balazki would never have helped. I'm . . . I'm sorry it's got to end like this. None of us wants to die. But we haven't any choice, have we?'

The professor adjusted his pince-nez, which were awry on his little nose. He put a hand on Radford's shoulder. 'No choice,' he agreed. 'But if we can wreck that launching ramp, the whole operation will be delayed for weeks, and in that time our nations will surely uncover the truth.'

Radford moved towards the open door. Holding on to a safety bar, he looked down. The powerful arc lights showed every detail in the ravine. Soldiers had already reached a group of high-mounted machine guns and were swinging the barrels towards the helicopter.

Now Radford glanced up. There was some light. Not much, but enough to show the ragged outline of the ravine top. They were almost level with it and still ascending in a straight line.

Radford shouted to Peter: 'Start flying forward! I'll tell you when we're directly over the ramp!'

The pitch of the main screw changed.

The helicopter continued to rise, but not so quickly, for it was moving north at the same time.

Streaks of vivid light soared towards them. They passed behind the tail of the machine. Radford mumbled to himself: 'Tracer bullets.'

At first, he was surprised by what he thought to be bad aiming. Then he realised that the gunners below were at a disadvantage, for to them the helicopter was flying in almost total darkness. But even so, it could only be moments before crisscross traversing fire would find them.

They were slightly above the top edges of the ravine. And almost — but not quite — directly over the ramp. It showed from far below as little more than a toy-like structure of thin steel. Yet Radford knew that it had massive strength. To ensure its total destruction, the helicopter must fall squarely on it.

'A bit more to the right!' Radford called to Peter.

With what seemed to be agonising slowness, Peter began to manoeuvre to the exact position. And Radford found himself anticipating the next ghastly moments — the moments when Peter suddenly cut dead the motors. The helicopter would drop like a great stone — or like a lift with a snapped cable.

There would be a nightmare of waiting while they clung to the falling machine. Then the end would come. There were two consolations — they would die instantly, and those hideous missiles would not rise on their missions of evil.

His brooding was interrupted when he saw an intricate web of tracer bullets. They were spraying towards them from the south end of the ravine. And they could not miss.

Radford shouted again to Peter: 'Quick, man! Move farther to the — '

It was then that the steel floor at his feet performed weird antics. Part of it curled up, as if being cut by a tin-opener, making a jagged hole. Another section disintegrated entirely as rivets broke loose and the plates broke free.

The whole helicopter shook like an animal coming out of water. Then it turned partly on its side and began what appeared to be an uncontrolled drift.

Radford had to cling with all his strength to the safety bar to save himself from being hurled through the open door. In the depth below, he glimpsed the ramp. They were moving away from it. Somehow, he managed to shout a warning to Peter. He heard Peter yell back a brief sentence. He could not hear all of it, but he picked up the words 'chipped prop.'

They were enough. He knew exactly what had happened. The main screw had been damaged, putting the helicopter entirely out of control. They were losing height — but only slowly. And the drift was taking them over the west side of the ravine.

Radford pressed himself against the window, and in that position he shuffled towards Peter and Tiere. Because of the crazy angle at which the machine was now flying, both men seemed to be hanging above him. Peter was fairly secure in his seat. But the professor was flat on the twisted floor.

Another shower of tracers closed round

the machine. It shook again, and as some of the lead glanced off there was a noise like a massed tattoo on kettle drums. Tiere gave a convulsive jerk. Then he looked in a surprised way at his right hand. Blood was coming from it.

It was at that moment that the main motor choked, then stopped.

For the smallest fraction of time the helicopter remained almost motionless in mid-air, as if fighting silently against a plunge to destruction. Then it fell.

Radford thought: *This is the end . . . and we've failed . . .*

He felt himself floating in space, with the roof of the machine below him. Professor Tiere's body brushed against him. He glimpsed Peter. The American was hanging like a fly to the backrest of his seat.

There was a hollow crash. It echoed like vile, unearthly music. At the same time, Radford realised in a strangely calm way that he had been thrown against the rear partition and that a pile of loose baggage had fallen across his legs. There was a whistling in his ears and a sticky feeling in his nostrils.

But the machine was no longer falling. Neither was it still. It was swaying very gently — just an inch or two from side to side.

Radford wiped blood from his nose. Then he tried to get to his feet. But Peter's voice made him freeze rigid.

'Don't move!' Peter was shouting. 'Whatever happens, don't move yet!'

'Why? We're all right. We must have landed on the side of the ravine!'

'We're on the side okay,' Peter said. He was sprawled across the width of the machine, face close to a gaping hole in the floor. But he was making no attempt to shift his position. He added harshly: 'We're balancing on the very edge of it! If you as much as cough, it could mean curtains for us!'

Very slowly, Radford turned his head and looked through a shattered window. Peter was not exaggerating. The wrecked helicopter was poised over the ravine as delicately as an acrobat. A few ounces of extra weight on the wrong side and it would overbalance, to plunge hundreds of feet into the dark abyss.

Radford absorbed the ghastly fact. It had been bad enough to think of a death fall which served a good purpose. It was infinitely worse to contemplate the same end when it could only serve their enemies.

He noticed Tiere. The professor was huddled in a corner farthest from the ravine and seemed to be conscious, but dazed. It was his weight, more than anyone else's, which was preventing the machine dropping.

Radford called: 'Stay right where you are, Professor!'

Tiere understood. He nodded. But a moment later he started to grope for his pince-nez. The helicopter dipped heavily over the ravine. Peter gave a loud sigh to relieve his stretched nerves. After a couple of fear-laden seconds, it swung back.

It was a waking nightmare. Obviously, the bottom of the wreckage had found the finest possible point of balance on some small rocky pinnacle. Anything — even a slight change in wind direction — could upset that balance and topple them to destruction.

In theory, Radford and Peter had only

to shift over to the same side as the professor, then get out quickly. But the facts were much more complicated. An initial thrust was always required to begin any bodily movement. That alone would be enough to invite immediate disaster.

Peter said: 'This sure is some spot! It looks like we'll have to end our time right here, breathing softly and keeping good and still!'

Radford wondered whether he could safely toss some of the fallen baggage to the side of the machine. He had almost decided to take the risk when a sharp series of crashes shook the whole tortured structure. The roof immediately below the main engine mounting twisted in the same way that the floor had done. Slashes of fire from tracers cut through one side of the helicopter and out of the other.

At the same time, the wreckage moved. It shifted a full foot away from the sheer drop, and there was a grating sound of rock against steel plates. Then it spun in a half-circle, dipped its nose, and finally righted itself in almost a normal position.

Unwittingly, the gunners in the ravine

had saved them. They had again opened fire on the helpless helicopter, and the massed impact of bullets had been more than enough to tilt it away from the edge and start the slide off the pinnacle.

The professor wrenched open the door at his side. At the same time, he winced with pain from his wounded hand. Then, pince-nez once more clipped to his nose, he looked for a ladder.

'Never mind that!' Radford told him. 'This crate could explode any time, with these tracers flying around! Jump for it!'

It was a seven-foot jump — a long way for the professor to fall. He hit the ground heavily and rolled into a cluster of cacti, but did not injure himself. Peter and Red followed, landing lightly.

The ground here consisted of small rocks jutting out of stretches of sand. To the north it sloped downwards, broken by occasional high peaks. The lowering sun was bathing everywhere with a deep red glow, making the desolation almost beautiful. But none of them had the time to appreciate scenery. Standing a full twenty yards from the ravine, they were safe from the machine guns far below. But the top of the helicopter was still within range. They watched with dejected fascination as tracers ripped into the main motor. Then the expected happened. There was a boom from somewhere deep inside the mangled machine. It became a white-hot pyre, flame and smoke licking a hundred feet into the air. They had to fall back still farther to escape the fierce heat blast.

The blaze did not last for long. A couple of minutes was enough to reduce the helicopter to a skeleton of glowing girders.

Peter was the first to break their heavy silence. He said: 'There goes around half a million dollars of Uncle Sam's dough.'

'Uncle Sam can stand the loss,' Radford said. 'But can we? There was food and water in there — enough to keep us alive for a few days. But now we've nothing.'

Peter jerked his huge shoulders. 'I figure Balazki's men will finish us before we've time to die of thirst or starvation.'

'I don't think they'll bother about us anymore,' Radford told him.

'You don't? Why?'

'Because with night coming on, we

could play a good game of hide-and-seek among these rocks. It might take them days to find us. And why should they go to that trouble? What harm can we do them now? They'll know that we haven't even been able to try to put out a radio SOS. Down there, Balazki, Goerler and the rest of them must be feeling relieved and contented. There's nothing to stop them firing the rockets on schedule.'

Professor Tiere was wrapping a handkerchief round his hand where a bullet had grazed the flesh under the thumb. He said morosely: 'We'll get a very good view of the rockets when they take off. We'll . . . we'll see the beginning of a terrible crime against humanity! *Sacré!* It makes me feel ill!'

Radford looked at his wristwatch. 'The way things are, we won't have so long to wait. Just under four and a half hours, in fact. Four and a half hours — then tens of thousands will die and probably freedom in Europe will die, too. It's not a pretty thought.'

'If only I'd had a few more seconds,' Peter said. 'That'd have been enough for me to get over the ramp. I was almost there. I guess I was scared all right. No one wants to get himself killed. But it would have been worth it.'

Professor Tiere had just finished knotting his improvised bandage with the aid of his teeth. 'Since there's nothing we can do, we might as well rest,' he said. 'Let us at least get a little farther away from the ravine. Those . . . those criminals of the Black Legion might come up here just to look at the wreckage of the helicopter, then we'll be found.'

Radford nodded agreement. There was no point in remaining where they were and risking recapture. They were helpless and defeated, but they might as well remain free during the short time left before the nuclear attacks.

Then suddenly Radford did something which contrasted with his usual calm. He gave a shout.

'Wait! We've been forgetting something!'

Peter gave an indifferent grunt. 'Then let's keep it that way,' he said. 'The way I feel right now, I'd like to be able to forget everything!'

Radford ignored him. 'What about the airstrip?' he asked. 'The place Balazki told us about, where the transport planes landed?'

Professor Tiere cocked his head to one side, looking at Red with puzzled curiosity. 'But what of it indeed? Balazki said there was a natural airstrip about a mile west of the ravine. We all noted the fact, but — '

'There may be aircraft on it at this moment!' Radford interrupted. 'It's just possible that we might be able to seize one of them!'

There was a brief silence while they looked at each other. Then Peter said: 'You figure we could use one of them to have another go at the launching ramp?'

'You've got the idea.'

'But *if* any planes are there, they're sure to be well guarded.'

'Not necessarily. My guess is that they'll be there to evacuate the ravine as soon as the rockets have been launched. They have no reason to think they're in any danger, so why should they put a strong guard over them? And Balazki won't suspect that we'll make our way there, because it's a mad thing to do. But sometimes it's the mad things which succeed, because nobody expects them.'

Professor Tiere looked uncertain. 'There's sure to be some people there, *mon ami*. There are only three of us, with one Luger between us. What can we expect to do against such odds? Anyway, we may not find the airstrip for many hours. Not, perhaps, till too late.'

'I've thought of those difficulties,' Radford said. 'They are real enough. But it's better to try the next-to-impossible than to wander about doing nothing.'

'You're right,' Peter said. 'I'm for finding that airstrip.'

Tiere smiled. 'No Frenchman ever refused a challenge. Whatever happens, nothing can be worse than it is now, so let's move west.'

The decision was reached, but they did not move immediately. Radford spent several minutes studying the gaunt landscape.

There was no reason to doubt Balazki's statement that the airstrip lay about a mile to the west — the side of the ravine, in fact, on which they were now standing. The problem was to locate it as quickly as possible. They did not have time to waste in floundering amid the crevasses and peaks. The obvious answer was to climb one of the pinnacles and hope that the airstrip would be visible from the extra height. But such a climb would be a long and probably dangerous business. There must be another clue to the precise direction . . .

A sudden thought struck Radford. He put it into words. 'All the equipment which has been flown in must have been manhandled to the ravine,' he said. 'So they must have cleared some sort of path through all these rocks which will lead us direct to the airstrip.'

He had scarcely finished speaking when Peter said: 'I think I see it!'

Peter was pointing to the south end of the ravine. A ribbon-like track was only just discernible. It was visible for about half a mile, vanishing into the centre of a long and high ridge.

Radford said: 'There are no obstructions on it that I can see. It *must* have been artificially cleared. That will be it! If we follow that path, the chances are we'll arrive right at the place we want.'

'Okay man — let's go!'

But Radford shook his head. 'Not quite so fast. Remember, some of Balazki's men may be out looking for us, so we have to be careful. When we get to the path, we won't actually move along it. Instead, we'll keep among the rocks at the side. They're fairly big and ought to give us good cover.'

Within ten minutes they were following the direction of the path towards the ridge. It was not easy going, for Radford's insistence on caution meant that they had to make frequent short detours to remain concealed. But their glimpses of the path surface convinced them that they were moving in the right direction. The dusty surface bore marks of many feet and the tracks made by small wheeled vehicles.

When they reached the ridge, they saw that the path led through a narrow opening between two high shoulders of rock. They moved along it quickly.

At the other side of the ridge they

stopped. The path wound on, sloping downward. Beyond it was the vast level expanse of which Balazki had spoken. It shimmered dark yellow in the evening sun. At one side of it, nearest to them, stood five four-engine freighter planes, each roughly camouflaged with brown netting. Nothing else was to be seen — not a tent, not a man.

Peter gave a low whistle. 'There's no guard at all,' he said. 'Those crates are just waiting to fly the Balazki mob out of here. This looks like it'll be easy!'

'I'm not so sure things are so easy,' Radford said.

'Why? This is what you expected!'

'I expected to find aircraft here and I didn't think there'd be a large guard over them. But I thought we'd find a few soldiers — and I still do.'

'But where are they?'

'Probably inside one of the planes. There's no reason for them to stay in the open, so they're likely to be relaxing in comfort.'

Professor Tiere, who was breathing heavily after his exertions, said: 'If that is so, they will have seen us, *oui*?'

'I don't think so — there's still plenty of rock in front of us, and the scenery isn't so beautiful that they'll want to keep looking out of the windows. My guess is that they're either sleeping or playing cards.'

'Then what now?' Peter asked.

'We'll creep up to the edge of the airstrip and take a closer look at those planes — then we'll decide how to get to work.'

The path offered a quick route to the perimeter of the natural airstrip. But to use it would invite detection from anyone in the planes. So, sometimes bending double and sometimes crawling, they again moved forward. During a brief pause Radford again looked at his watch. It was fifteen minutes to six.

★   ★   ★

And in Paris, at the Defence Ministry . . .

General Phillipe said to his aide: 'It's a quarter to six, and still no report from Sidi bel Abbes.'

The aide was watching the deputy chief of staff carefully. It was an important part of his job to study the general's whims and moods. Particularly his moods. At the moment the general showed all the signs of building up into a raging temper. Not that he could be blamed on this occasion.

'Sidi bel Abbes said they'd put in a call to us as soon as they heard anything,' the aide said reassuringly. 'If anything more had gone wrong, you'd have heard before now.'

'I'm not so sure!' General Phillipe snapped. 'It's hours since we were told of the second explosion at Fort Allengrah. Hours since Captain Radford and the others were given permission to make a reconnaissance in the helicopter. Since then, there's been the most complete silence! Meantime, the government is meeting! They'll be asking questions and expecting me to provide the answers!'

General Phillipe stamped to his wall map, glared at it, then said: 'This is intolerable! Put a call through to Sidi bel Abbes. I'll speak to the G.O.C. myself.'

Five minutes later, the deputy chief of staff in Paris and the general officer commanding in North Africa were talking over more than a thousand miles of telephone wire.

'There's been no news at all from the helicopter,' the G.O.C. said.

'Perhaps they have run out of fuel?'

'That's possible, but I'd have expected them to send a radio signal for help.'

'I suppose they could have had engine trouble.'

'*Oui*, it's another possibility. I've been thinking that if they've had to come down on the plateau, they might not be able to use their radio.'

There was a long pause, then General Phillipe said: 'You mean because of the mountains?'

'Exactly. They could make short wave transmission impossible. I could send out a bomber squadron to look for them, but they would not reach the plateau area before dark. In any case, it is almost impossible to see much while flying over that country, because the peaks make it too dangerous to fly low.'

General Phillipe ran fingers through his grey hair. 'You realise we'll have an extra crisis on our hands if the helicopter is lost, too. For one thing, it's a United States machine and has an American pilot. Washington will be very disturbed. So will the British government over the loss of one of their best agents. And we can't afford to lose Professor Tiere.'

The G.O.C.'s voice was heavy with concern as he said: 'I take the blame. It was my decision to let them go.'

But General Phillipe, despite his occasional burst of temper, was not the sort of officer to avoid responsibility.

'That's absurd!' he said. 'Your decision was correct. It has my full approval. Any risks were unavoidable.' He hesitated, then asked: 'What's happening at the site of Fort Allengrah?'

'I've carried out your orders. I've not attempted to land any more people there in case there's another missile explosion. But bombers have flown over the area to make a survey. It's exactly as Captain Radford described it — nothing left alive.'

General Phillipe sighed. 'It seems that

all we can do for the moment is wait,' he said.

'*Oui* — wait and hope that Captain Radford is still working for us . . . '

7

Airstrip Emergency

They were crouching behind a rock with the nearest of the planes less than ten yards away. They could see through the round windows of all of the machines. There was no sign of life. No sound or movement. But that was not all. The desolation of the place could also be felt instinctively. It was something which pressed into blood and bones.

Peter whispered: 'If any soldiers are around, they must be the slackest outfit on earth!'

Radford's forehead was creased with uncertainty. 'I can't understand it,' he said. 'I'd expect to see shadows from men inside the aircraft, but there's nothing. Yet I can't believe that Balazki would leave them entirely unprotected.'

'Well, that's just what he's done, bud. Seems like he's been a bit too confident.

Let's walk right up to them and — '

'We'll do nothing of the sort — not yet. This could be a trap.'

'You mean . . . there might be guards here and they might have seen us?'

'That's just what I mean. I'm not convinced about it, but I've got to make sure. You two keep yourselves under cover while I make a test.'

Slowly, Radford raised his head above the rock until he must have been easily visible to anyone inside the planes.

Professor Tiere hissed: '*Sacré* — be careful!'

Peter tried to pull him down, but Red pushed him away. Nothing happened. Still not a flicker of movement from within those windows.

Radford picked up a stone. It was large and heavy, comfortably filling the whole palm of his hand. He hurled it at the nearest plane. It flew through the open mesh of the camouflage net, just grazing one side of it, and slammed against the side of the plane close to the main door. There was a clatter from the thin steel plate. But no other reaction.

'That proves it,' Peter said, standing too. 'There's not a soul here. We're okay.'

Radford was silent for a few seconds. Then he said: 'I agree with you — except I'm not so sure about us being okay.'

'What do you mean? Let's not hang around! This is our chance to get inside one of those crates and wreck the launching ramp. I guess I'll fix the second try at a crash landing without trouble.'

'You're a lot too impetuous,' Radford told him, picking up another stone. 'Watch.'

The second stone whistled through the air. Again it touched part of the camouflage net before hitting the plane.

'So what?' Peter asked. 'It's the same as before.'

'That's exactly what I mean.'

'Quit talking in riddles, will you! What *do* you mean?'

It was Tiere who provided part of the answer. He said excitedly: 'The net! It's vibrating!'

A small part of the material was shaking from the impact of the stone. All of them watched until it ceased.

132

'Camouflage net is usually made of cord,' Radford said. 'That stuff is coloured wire — fairly thick wire by the look of it.'

Peter said doubtfully: 'I guess that's unusual, but what's it supposed to prove?'

For an answer, Radford walked into the open. Gazing at the ground, he passed behind the first two planes. Then he pointed at the smooth rock surface.

'There's more wire here — only this is extra thick. In fact, it looks to me like high-voltage cable.'

Peter flipped up a cigarette from a paper packet. There was a shake in his voice as he said: 'So the netting's electrified!'

'That's about it. The current must be fed from storage batteries in the ravine.'

'Yeah, but those batteries must be low-tension, and they'd never harm anyone.'

'True, but the voltage can easily be stepped up by transformers. My guess is that if we touch this netting we'll fry to death!'

Now all of them were standing over the main lead cable. It was more than two inches thick, its outer cover heavily armoured. Thinner cables sprouted from it, joining to each of the nets covering the five massive aircraft. There were places where those nets did not quite reach the ground, and Peter pointed it out.

'We're not licked yet,' he said. 'We can crawl underneath!'

'We can,' Radford agreed. 'But what can we do after that? If current's flowing through the netting, it must be circulating the steel plates of the planes, too. We'd be electrocuted as soon as we tried to touch a door. And even if the plates were non-conductors, which they're not, you couldn't start the motors with all that wire over the propeller blades.'

Peter nodded in reluctant agreement. 'Balazki's scientists sure do work thoroughly,' he said. 'No wonder they don't have soldiers here — there's no need for them.'

Radford turned to Professor Tiere and said: 'Do you think there's any way we can break the current?'

Tiere was bending down, examining the joins which linked the thinner cables to the nets. He shook his head as he did so. Then he abruptly straightened and made one of his typical Gallic gestures, throwing up his arms.

'But of course there may be a way! Why didn't I think of it immediately? You have a pistol, *capitaine*, so perhaps you can shoot through the cable!'

Radford thought for a moment, then said: 'Yes, I daresay that's possible.'

Peter looked at Radford indignantly. 'What's on your mind now?' he asked. 'It's a good idea and I don't see how it can fail. A slug ought to slice through that stuff easily enough.'

'I hope you're right,' Radford said. 'Anyway, we'll soon know.' Then he asked Tiere: 'Is it safe to touch it?'

'*Oui*, all the leads are insulated as well as armoured. It's only the netting which is deadly.'

Radford picked up the main cable at the point where the thinner leads spread out of it. All of them were round, smooth, and very tough. He took out the Luger. With the muzzle less than an inch from one of the fine leads, he squeezed the trigger. There was a bark which echoed faintly against the ridge. The cable convulsed like a snake, then settled. A few chips of rock flew into the air, one of them hitting Radford's chest, and there was a small eddy of dust.

But the electrical lead remained unharmed, save for a scratch down one side of it.

'You're not shooting so good,' Peter said.

'It was a direct hit,' Radford told him. 'No one could miss at that range. The bullet just glanced off because the cable's round and hard. It's exactly what I suspected would happen.'

'It must have a heck of a hard outer cover.'

'One of the new fragmentation-proof plastics by the look of it.'

Tiere said: 'Then we are beaten — we cannot cut the current.'

Radford said very softly: 'You're wrong there, Professor. We can. It can be done by shooting through it.'

Perplexed, they gazed at him. Peter said: 'But you've just said you *can't* shoot through it! We've seen that you can't! Now you say you can ... who's going crazy around here?'

Radford gave a taut smile. 'None of us, I hope. Now listen to me carefully — the bullet was deflected because it was moving in free space when it hit the round surface. It was natural for it to be knocked off course. You understand me?'

'Yeah, that's clear enough.'

'But a bullet *will* go through it if the muzzle is pressed against the surface at the moment of firing. Shoot that way and the bullet must continue straight down because the barrel prevents it being deflected.'

Peter flexed his big shoulders and said: 'Of course. That's what you ought to have done the first time. Go right . . . '

Professor Tiere sprang forward. His face had changed — it was pallid.

'You'll die if you do it that way!' he gasped. 'You talk of firing with the gun muzzle pressed against the cable . . . think what that means! The bullet will cut through the insulation. Immediately an electrical contact will be formed through the pistol to you! The shock may only last a fraction of a second . . . but it will be more than enough!'

Radford said flatly: 'I know all that.'

'Then why even think of such a plan?'

'Because we *must* get one of these planes in the air if we're to wreck the rocket ramp, and it's the only way to do it.'

'And you're prepared to die to break off the current?'

Radford shrugged. 'Does it matter? Does it really make any difference? Peter will have to fly the plane — that's his particular job. He'll be killed when he crashes on the ramp. Only a matter of a few minutes will divide us. In any case, we're all living on borrowed time, because if things had gone right in the helicopter we'd all be dead by now.'

There was a heavy quiet. Then Tiere said: 'I think Peter would rather have you with him than me. You will be better company for him in the plane . . . so I will shoot through the cable.'

Radford gave an emphatic shake of his head. 'The way things have turned out, there's no need for you to die at all, Professor. I'll break the cable. Peter will crash the plane. And you will stay right here. Once Peter's in the air, he'll be able to flash a quick signal to Sidi bel Abbes before he makes for the ravine, so you ought to be rescued within a day.'

'*Ciel!* Why should an old man such as I live while — '

'Because there's never any point in dying needlessly. In your case it would be a terrible waste, Professor. You're a brilliant scientist and you can continue to do a lot of good for a lot of people. But that's not all — you can be the man to let the world know what really happened out here. You can answer all the questions and make sure that nothing like this can ever happen again. That's a vital duty.'

There was no arguing with Radford's flat logic. Tiere said in hoarse tones: 'So I must watch you kill yourself here, Hugh. Then watch Peter fly away to his death.'

'Don't watch, Professor. Get among the rocks and stay there, it'll be easier that way. There's no sense in making a morbid ritual out of this — anyway, we haven't the time to spare. I'll cut the cable now.'

Radford knelt on one leg. He pressed

the muzzle against the hard round surface. His face was pale and his lips stretched
tight.

Something exploded immediately in
front of him. Exploded gently, with little
more noise than a breath of wind.
Radford saw a grey-white cloud rise from
the ground. It rose fast, spreading at the
same time. Suddenly, before he could
back away, the cloud was enveloping him.

Then it vanished. In its place was a blur
of pink. Just pink everywhere. Vaguely, he
heard Tiere shout something and Peter
yell a reply. A sharp pain clutched at
Red's lungs and he began coughing.

It was then that he knew. He knew by
the pear-drop smell, by the fact that his
eyes were tight shut and he could not
open them, by the rawness in his chest.

This was gas. Tear gas. A grenade of the
stuff had been tossed at them.

Already a dozen questions were rushing
through his mind. But he thrust them
aside. Now, while blinded, every atom of
his mental power must be directed at
survival. That meant getting into clean
air. Moving as fast as possible from this

place. But he was close — very close — to the netting. A single step in the wrong direction . . .

The netting had been behind him when he knelt over the cable. He had not shifted. There had been clear space to left and right, the rocks in front. That must still be so.

Radford turned deliberately to his left and ran several staggering paces. The pain in his lungs lessened. With the fingers of his left hand he forced up his eyelids. They stayed open, but at first it was like staring through a bowl of heaving water. All was distorted, although the main outlines were clear. Four men were advancing down the path leading from the ridge. They were in the false Legion uniforms. And they carried rifles.

Carried rifles, but they were not attempting to use them. Why?

The answer came to Radford as soon as he realised that he was standing directly between the soldiers and the aircraft. Shots fired at him — or at Tiere and Peter — might damage the machines. There would be a fragment of extra safety if they could get between the aircraft. At least that would offer brief concealment and give them a chance to think.

Radford wiped streaming moisture from his eyes and looked towards Tiere and Peter. They were swaying and floundering, arms over their faces, the gas cloud still drifting around them. They must be guided out of it. But how? Radford knew that if he went to them, he would again become helpless himself. He made another lightning decision, bent almost double, and forced himself into another paroxysm of coughing as if the gas were still affecting his lungs. As if he were powerless because of it. And he rubbed his eyes, hoping to make the soldiers believe that blindness had returned.

But he was looking at the aircraft. They were standing in a straight line, tails towards the rocks and about ten feet separating their giant wing tips. Tiere and Peter were almost directly behind the first two.

Radford began moving in short, reeling steps. But they had a precise purpose. They took him round the front of the nearest planes. Then between them, with the draping nets on either side. Now, with the mountainous fuselages towering above him, he was temporarily concealed from the four soldiers. He ran down the space formed by the two aircraft until he reached the tail fins. He shouted to Tiere and Peter: 'This way! Follow the sound of my voice!'

They wavered, eyes closed and spluttering. Then they staggered in what was very roughly Radford's direction. It was sufficient to take them out of the thickest of the gas. But if they continued, they would almost certainly stumble into the netting. Radford again resumed his pose of being almost helpless. Coughing, swaying, he emerged into full view of the soldiers. Then he grabbed Tiere's arm. A second later, he had a grip on Peter's shoulder. Quickly but gently, he guided them into the space between the two aircraft.

Both were recovering. Peter was the first to open his bloodshot eyes. 'What . . . what was it?' he breathed.

Radford told him and added: 'It looks to me as if those soldiers only arrived on a routine check. If Balazki had thought we were here, he'd have sent more than four men and he'd probably have been himself.'

'It . . . it's kind of queer about those gas grenades.'

'From their angle, it's sensible. Their only real worry must be a chance visit by curious Arabs, and tear gas is a good way of overpowering them without risk to the aircraft.'

As he finished speaking, Radford looked round the angle of a tail fin. One of the soldiers was returning along the path at a run. Already he was almost at the ridge. There could be no doubt about his purpose — he was about to raise the alarm at the ravine. The three others were crouched behind a rock. Their heads and shoulders could be seen and they were gazing steadily towards the planes.

Radford said: 'It seems they'll be content to keep us here till help arrives, and that'll be in about twenty minutes.'

'Then we're trapped,' Peter said. 'If we move out of the cover of these crates, they'll either shoot us, or let us have another whiff of gas.'

Radford looked at the Luger which he still held in his right hand. It was a puny weapon against rifles and gas grenades, except at very short range. And certainly the soldiers would not allow the range to shorten. They could deal with any move by Radford, Peter and Tiere from where they were.

Or could they?

Radford noted the fact that only a few yards of open space separated them from the rocks at the edge of the airstrip. Suppose they made a dash for that cover? They would almost certainly make it without being picked off by Lebel fire, for they would be exposed for three or four seconds at the most.

But once under cover — what then? If they stood up to run for freedom, they would be shot. If they remained hugging the ground, another gas grenade would be thrown among them.

Those gas grenades . . .

They were of the impact type. The thin casing broke on striking any hard surface, releasing a liquid which became gaseous on exposure to the atmosphere. They had only a very localised effect, and for that reason it was apparently not thought necessary for the soldiers to carry respirators. To throw them, a man had to stand upright and project them with a stiff elbow action, not unlike bowling a cricket ball.

The facts flicked through Radford's brain like statistics in a computer. And an answer to the crisis — a desperate but possible answer — presented itself.

He looked at Peter and Tiere. The American had fully recovered. But the Frenchman was still wheezing as he dried his pince-nez on a handkerchief.

'Listen,' Radford told them. 'In a couple of minutes you two are going to make a run for the rocks. I'll stay here. This is what I hope will happen . . . '

Radford lay flat on his stomach. His left arm was crooked in front of him and the long barrel of the Luger was resting on it as he sighted on the soldiers. Behind him, Peter and Tiere were bending forward like sprinters waiting for the start of a race.

'Are you ready?' Radford asked, keeping his gaze on his target.

'Just waiting for your word,' Peter said.

'You know which rock you're making for? You'll be safe enough so long as you don't hesitate.'

'We can't take our eyes off it, bud.'

'That's fine. *Move . . .* '

Radford heard a sudden clatter of boots behind him. He sensed but did not see Peter and Tiere rush across the short clearing. Behind the rock forty yards away, the soldiers leaned against the butts of their Lebels and the barrels swivelled. But no shot was fired. As Radford had expected, they did not have a chance to take aim. Already Peter and Tiere were behind cover.

One of the rifle barrels remained pointed to the area where the two men had dropped out of sight. The others turned again, this time to cover the open space.

Radford thought: *They're waiting for me to follow. I hope they don't wait too long.*

He was partly hidden by the tail and rear wheel of the plane in front of him. The double thickness of camouflage netting completed his concealment. Only if the soldiers happened to direct a long and careful stare at one precise spot would they have any chance of noticing his rigid form.

Faintly, Radford heard the soldiers talking. Then one of them stood up. He became fully exposed from the centre of the body. In one hand he was holding a gas grenade. Carefully, Radford aligned the sights of the Luger. At about forty yards, this was going to be a very difficult shot.

The soldier's arm swept back. In this moment he stood poised like a statue. Radford squeezed the trigger.

The Luger gave a slight upward jump. The toggle joint bent double and an empty cartridge case jumped out of the ejection slot. Above the crack of exploding cordite, Radford felt the breech-block returning into position with a new round. He prepared to shoot again. But it was not necessary.

The soldier carried the gas grenade partly forward, as if intent on throwing it despite the bullet in his chest. Then he crumpled sideways, letting the grenade drop from his fingers.

Radford saw it hit the rock. He saw the

instantaneous cloud of smoke. It rose and spread round the soldiers, and in the midst of it they reeled and staggered, just as Radford and the others had done few minutes before.

Dropping the Luger in his holster, Radford stood up. Peter and Tiere were already moving towards him.

'Magnificent!' Tiere said. 'You were right! It happened just as you planned, *mon ami.*'

'Maybe it did, but we're still no better off than when we arrived at this airstrip. Anyway, we'll have to worry about that later. Our next job's to get right away from this place before reinforcements arrive.'

Peter nodded. 'Sure — we haven't long. Let's go!'

At the other side of the airstrip, there was another fringe of rocks and pinnacles, remote and forbidding, like everywhere else on the plateau. But at least it was well away from the ravine. They ran towards it, Red and Peter helping Professor Tiere.

Within five minutes the airstrip was out of sight, shielded by the great crags. There was no need to hurry now. Immediate pursuit was unlikely. They picked their way between rocks and occasionally slithered down banks of sand. As they did so, they felt reaction set in. The sort of reaction which follows tension and complete failure.

Twice, in the face of next-to-impossible odds, they had seemed to be on the verge of wrecking the launching ramp. Twice their plans had miscarried. True, they had escaped from the ravine and were still free. But that escape and that freedom were worth less than nothing when balanced against the holocaust which Balazki and his men would unleash that day. A heavy depression settled over them as they moved aimlessly on.

The worst of the day's heat was long since over, and it would not be long before they felt the chill of the Sahara night. It looked as if thirst would add to their torment. They scarcely spoke.

They had covered nearly two miles when they unexpectedly entered a tiny gully which had a narrow opening at each end. The sides were composed of vast boulder formations. But midway along the gully, soft sand had drifted into a shallow cave. It looked a good place to rest. They dropped on to the sand and gazed with weary eyes at the ground. They remained absolutely silent.

It was only because of the silence that Radford's quick hearing detected a faint, indescribable sound. It might have been caused by two soft surfaces rubbing together. Or perhaps merely by a trick of the breeze.

Radford tensed, listening more carefully. He heard it again. It was clearer, closer.

Now Peter had picked it up, too. He looked hard at Radford and asked: 'Do they have wild animals in these parts?'

'Not many.'

'Well it sounds to me like we're being stalked, bud.'

Radford paused. Then he said slowly: 'We're being stalked all right, but not by wild beasts. Anyway, they're not the four-legged variety.' And he pointed casually to an entrance to the gully.

A group of tribesmen were standing there. About a dozen of them. Some were carrying aged muzzle-loading muskets. Others were gripping cruelly curved scimitars, their blades as keen as a surgeon's scalpel. All were bearded, their thickly folded *burnous* hiding the lower part of their lean, dark-hued faces. There was something blood-chilling about their eyes. They glittered with the raw essence of hatred.

'Berbers,' Radford said softly. 'Wild Berbers.'

Peter said: Maybe any company's better than none.'

'Not this sort of company. In this region the Berber tribesmen are completely untamed. They hate white people at any time and something tells me they hate us in a particular way.'

Slowly, the Berbers began moving towards them, their eyes unblinking. Brown fingers cocked the hammers of muskets and caressed the edges of scimitars. There was a ghastly finality about their approach.

Professor Tiere hissed: 'Use your Luger, *mon ami*! Try to frighten them away!'

Radford shook his head.

'Keep completely still!' he snapped. 'It's our only chance! I know what these people are like. If we try to move, we're finished!'

152

8

Locust-Eaters

As the Berbers advanced, they spread out. They formed a wide semi-circle round the shallow cave, cutting off all chance of retreat. Then they halted. The nearest of them were only a few yards away. Some were touching their lips with the tips of their tongues, as if savouring the slaughter to come.

Peter and Tiere gazed at them as if hypnotised. Radford was sprawled on his side, supporting himself on one elbow. It was costing a great effort, but he was managing to disguise the fear he felt. He knew that above all else he must not give way to panic. If they were to survive — and that seemed a remote possibility — a lot would depend on him, for he alone of the three could speak the Berber dialect.

Radford coughed loudly and deliber-ately, to break the tension. Then he said as confidently as he could: 'We have been hoping you would find us. We are your friends. We need your help.'

Some of the Berbers showed a hint of surprise at hearing Radford use their tongue. One of them, who seemed to be their leader, advanced a little farther until he stood over him.

'We shall help you to your graves,' he said.

Although it was the answer he had been expecting, Radford made a pretence of astonishment.

'I don't understand you! We have done you no harm!'

This was received with a rumble of infuriated voices. Scimitars waved menacingly.

'You lie and you have no courage!' The Berber leader spat out the words.

'My message is true. I assure you we are your friends. We — '

'You snivel about friendship when you fear our vengeance! I knew that the soldiers of France were infidels, but I learn today that they also are cowards!'

A sudden roar of agreement went up

from the others, and they pressed closer. Radford knew that to try further argument would be fatal. Somehow, he must gain time by getting the Berber to talk at length.

'Tell me why you hate us,' he said gently. 'We are helpless and you can indeed slay us. But we should know the reason before we feel your blades at our throats.'

'The reasons are as many as the grains of sand at your feet! All those with skins such as yours are enemies of our people. It has always been thus, and so it shall be till time ends. But have you not chosen to double the hate between us? Have you not added the foulest treachery to your many sins?'

Moving slowly, Radford got to his feet. He knocked grime from his tunic and set his *kepi* straight. 'I don't understand. You speak in riddles,' he said.

'They are not riddles to you, a captain of the Legion!'

'But they are,' Radford told him, keeping resentment out of his voice. 'We do not hate you and I know nothing of this treachery you talk about.'

'You lie skilfully, but it will gain you nought. Hear me — you legionnaires condemn those of us who trade in slaves. Yet you yourselves take our Arab people into slavery. What else is that than treachery?'

So there it was.

Radford realised that Balazki's swoop on the village had worked too well. Blame for the raid had been pinned firmly on the Legion. And why not? The whole outrage had been carried out by men in Legion uniforms. And it was a practical certainty that at least a handful of tribesmen had seen the wretched people being escorted to the ravine. The story must have swept the Sahara, along with the other tales of strange events in the Asben Plateau. No wonder that these Berbers spoke of even greater hatred for France.

Radford said: 'You talk of Gacruss village. I know what happened there, and it was a day of infamy. But know this — France and the Legion were not guilty of that.'

There was a rustle from the Berber's robe. His open hand streaked towards Radford's face. Radford saw the blow coming. He could have swayed away from it, or knocked the arm aside. But he chose to take its full force. He knew that if he avoided it, the Berbers would hold him in even greater contempt.

It was a hard blow, and as the Berber was wearing several ornate rings, it grazed his cheek. But he took it without flinching.

But Peter, despite the acute danger, showed all the normal American's dislike of not hitting back. He, too, got to his feet. He did so in a single bound.

'Say, we're not taking this!' he roared. 'So they're going to knife us, eh? Okay, but I aim to hand out some damage on my own account first!'

Before Radford could do or say anything, Peter had grasped the Berber round the waist. He showed his immense strength by lifting the man in the air as though he were a child. Then he threw him — threw him bodily so that the tribesman hurtled several feet through the air before crashing onto the sand in a confused mass of robes.

For seconds there was absolute stillness. Then a screech of fury went up from the Berbers.

Radford jerked the Luger from his holster. He had fired one shot in the ravine and two at the airstrip, leaving five rounds. With those, he could make the Berbers pay a heavy price. As he raised the pistol, he took first pressure on the trigger. The Berbers had been on the point of rushing forward. But they wavered at the sight of a high-precision weapon in the hand of a man who obviously had the skill and training to use it effectively. Even those with muskets dared not aim them, for they knew that the Luger would be fired first. And there was no chance of taking Red from the rear because his back was to the rocks.

Peter said: 'They're scared! They don't want to argue with the automatic, and I don't blame them.'

But Radford shook his head. 'Those men are tough and brave,' he said. 'They don't want to rush us, but if they have to they will.'

Their leader was getting off the

ground. His face was twitching under the strain of suppressed fury and humiliation. But at a swift glance, he understood why his tribesmen had not attacked. And apparently he was not inclined to set an example himself. He turned again to Radford.

'Our people are too few in number for me to let them die uselessly,' he said.

'You're wise,' Radford told him. 'We mean you no harm, so if you won't help us, I hope you'll leave us alone.'

'We do not help white infidels! Neither can we help those who take innocent people into slavery.' He broke off to point to Peter, then went on: 'That man who has the shoulders of an ox has chosen to degrade me. I seek a personal vengeance from him!'

'What sort of vengeance?'

'I say that we must fight, just he and I. Fight to the death.'

'And the weapons?'

The Berber felt under his robe and produced a nine-inch two-edged knife.

'Blades such as these,' he said. 'I, Yssaf the Younger, am famed among my people for my skill with the blade. I can kill the big man easily — and that is why I make a pledge to you. My pledge is that you will all be unharmed if he can kill me in this combat.'

Radford digested the challenge.

'And if you kill him?' he asked.

'Then the rest of you will die, too. Even your pistol will be useless against us — for we shall imprison you in this gully. We shall stand guard behind the rocks at each end and watch as you perish of thirst. If you try to break out, we shall shoot you. Perhaps, as your end draws near, you will choose to die by our bullets as a welcome end to your agony.'

Radford was thinking quickly. It was now plain that Peter's sudden fury had ended all chance of making peace with the Berbers. The only hope of survival was to win the knife fight. But the American's prospect of victory was practically nil. On the other hand, the Berbers were famous for their skill with cold steel. And this man Yssaf's boast that he was supreme among them was almost certainly a true one, for he would not otherwise have made it in front of the others.

Only a short time before, all three of them had accepted the prospect of dying. There had seemed to be no point in carrying on since they had failed to wreck the rocket ramp. But now Radford realised that he, at least, had recovered from the first shock effect of that failure. He wanted to live. Wanted to seek some other way of preventing the disaster. Hope would only be dead if they were to die, too.

So Yssaf's challenge must be accepted. And Yssaf must be defeated.

But it definitely could not be done by Peter. The American had the courage of a lion and would not flinch from the fight. But he would be doomed from the first moment — and his friends with him.

Radford told himself: *This is something I'll have to try to handle.*

He put his own chances in such a duel at about fifty-fifty at the best. His training as an agent had taken in all forms of deadly combat, including use of the knife. But he did not handle a killing blade every day. The Berbers did.

161

He said to Yssaf: 'I will fight you.'

Yssaf shook his head. 'It is the other man whom I shall meet. It was he who threw me. On him I shall have my vengeance.'

'But he knows nothing of knife fighting.'

'What do I care of that? I shall see fear in his eyes and I shall laugh.'

Radford tried a different approach. 'It seems, Yssaf, that you are a coward! You are afraid to meet one such as I! For I, too, am skilled with the knife. But you are glad to challenge a man who has no chance!'

The taunt worked immediately. Yssaf gathered his robe about him and tilted back his bearded chin. 'You dare to name me a coward! If you wish to fight for your friend, it is well with me. I shall slay you, just as I would slay him!'

Neither Peter nor Tiere had been able to understand a word of Radford's talk with the Berber, but they could guess a lot. Peter, who was straining to use his huge fists, suddenly asked: 'Say, what gives? Is that Arab looking for a personal settlement with me?'

Radford had to avoid the truth, knowing that Peter would never allow anyone to deputise for him if he knew what had been happening.

'The settling's to be with me,' Radford said. 'We're to have a little tussle with knives.'

'Knives! Okay, if that's how he wants it, I'll take him on. It's me he has the grudge against.'

'He'd rather fight *me*,' Radford said with careful emphasis.

'But why? I'm the — '

'It's all fixed, Peter. He says he's a champion, and I've told him I know a thing or two about the business myself.'

Professor Tiere looked at Radford with anxious eyes. 'Would it not be better to use the gun to try to get away?'

'It would not, Professor. I might kill several of them, but they'd soon swamp us. This is our only hope. If I can win the fight, they'll not harm us. They've promised that.'

'But can we trust their promise? *Tiens!*'

'I think we can trust them. Anyway, we've no choice about it.'

Radford knew that the Berber people varied greatly in their standards of honour. Those who lived in the large towns were often entirely unscrupulous. But in the remote areas, their word could usually be relied upon.

They were an unusual and very ancient race, spread over almost all of North Africa. Four hundred years before Christ, the Greek historian Herodotus had written of them: 'They let their hair grow long, and when they catch any vermin on their persons, they bite them and throw them away.' Herodotus also described their habit of flavouring some of their food with dried locusts. This they still did when food was short, and so they were often known as 'locust eaters'.

But mainly they were famed for their ferocity in battle. They were fantastically brave and utterly cruel. In some areas they co-operated in a lukewarm way with the French. But in others, such as this Asben region, it seemed that nothing could change their anti-white feelings. They were the only people still capable of full-scale tribal rebellions. As recently as 1953, thousands of Berbers had stormed out of the Atlas Mountains on to small towns and villages, slaughtering hundreds of French people and peaceful Arabs. But they were quickly encircled and defeated by units of the Foreign Legion. The leaders of the rebellion were executed and all the others forced to give up their arms.

Yes, they were a strange race, the Berbers. A race to be feared.

Yssaf was speaking again. He said to Radford: 'We shall not delay, for night will soon be upon us. Choose a blade.'

Some of the Berbers pulled knives from their sashes. They held them towards Radford. He selected one which was short, straight, and worn thin with constant sharpening. Despite its obvious age, it was a superbly balanced weapon, and the black ebony haft fitted naturally into the hand.

Now the Berbers formed a wide circle in the gully. They spoke eagerly to each other, anticipating the amusement to come. Yssaf was pulling the top of his robe from his shoulders and tucking it into the waist, leaving his torso naked. He also took off his *burnous*, revealing long, greasy black hair. He was well-muscled, suggesting the agile strength of a wildcat.

Radford removed his *kepi* and tunic. Then he unknotted his necktie and opened the collar of his shirt. But he kept the shirt on. It would give some protection against a fall on the sharp, coarse sand, which could cause acute pain if embedded in the skin. Yssaf did not need to take such a precaution. Being a Berber, his skin had a natural leathery toughness.

Peter had taken over the Luger. He looked at it, then at Radford. 'I don't like this,' he said. 'I've a hunch I ought to be waving that knife around.'

Radford smiled indulgently at his American friend. 'Just waving it about wouldn't do much good,' he said. 'Using a blade's not my natural way of fighting, or yours, but I know enough about it to tell you it takes a lot of skill.'

Peter said: 'If it starts to look like you're going to come off the worse out of this, I'll move in and . . . '

Radford put a hand on Peter's shoulder. 'That'd be crazy,' he said. 'Keep right out of this and leave it to me.'

Yssaf called from the opposite side of the gully: 'The time is come! I shall cut you into pieces, Captain! I shall hear you scream for mercy, but there is no mercy in me!' He started towards Radford.

An expert at anything can be recognised at a glance. There is a refined competence about the way he moves. And almost always there is a certain grace about him, a sureness of touch. Yssaf was no exception. From his first forward step, it became clear that he was a master of knife fighting.

He came at a semi-crouch, head and shoulders well forward. The novice, when trying to use a knife, holds the weapon high for a downward stab, which is easy to avoid. But Yssaf's blade was held correctly. It was slightly in front of the centre of his stomach, ready for an upward plunge. His sandalled feet padded softly and easily. In his eyes there was gloating expectation.

In those critical seconds before they clashed, Radford tasted the stark dread of one who faces a nearly hopeless struggle. But the spasm of fear was over in a moment. It was replaced by concentration on the Berber.

167

Radford's own stance as he advanced was a little different to that of Yssaf. He was slightly more upright, so as to be able to turn and sway more easily. He knew that his main asset was his very fast reflexes. He could act faster than thought. His tactics must be to avoid Yssaf's thrusts and try to get in a counter-stab while the Berber was off balance.

But Yssaf did not attack immediately. When the two were just out of reach, he made a lightning movement, switching his knife to his left hand. At the same time, he began circling to the left. This compelled Radford to circle in the same direction. That also put him in an unexpected difficulty. As his weapon was in his right hand, he would be forced to make any thrust in an outwards direction, which was both unnatural and difficult. But the Berber, who apparently could use both hands equally well, faced no such problem, now that the knife was in his left hand. He would be able to stab at the much easier inward angle. He was making cunning use of the fact that he was ambidextrous.

They made three complete circles. The

only sound was the sighing of the evening wind and the heavy breathing of the two men.

Then it came. Yssaf attacked.

He did two things at the same time. He quickened his sideways movement, and he came forward half a pace. It was done with the smooth speed of travelling quicksilver. And his knife was streaking forward and up, aimed at a point just below the centre of Radford's chest bone.

But Radford had moved, too. Not all of him — only the top half of his body. He was bending to his right from the waist. The glittering steel passed over his ribs and a full inch clear of them.

The swiftness of Radford's evasive move surprised Yssaf. He had expected his blade to meet flesh and bone. Instead, it contacted only empty air, and he continued to move forward. Radford abruptly straightened his body. The shoulders of the two men crashed against each other. The result for Yssaf was inevitable. He spun round, lost his balance and fell on his back.

Radford's instinct was to throw himself on Yssaf. But he resisted the temptation.

He knew that a man on his back and fully conscious had many advantages against an adversary who was foolish enough to try dropping on him. It looked as if Yssaf was hoping for Radford to make just such a move, for he remained perfectly still for several seconds — almost inviting the attack.

But Radford stood back. Not far enough back . . .

Yssaf's right hand streaked out. His fingers clasped Radford's left foot above the ankle. He gave a sudden and powerful pull. Radford felt his leg being jerked forward and knew that through momentary carelessness, he had avoided one mistake only to make another. He felt a sickening jolt through his spine as he hit the sand.

Yssaf was still holding on to the leg. He was shifting his grip and twisting the foot in a way which could end only in a broken joint — unless Radford made the correct counter-move. The counter-move here — as in the case of many close combat holds — was to give way to the point of pressure. Impulse made people resist such holds, which only added to their effect. But a complete lack of resistance often made them useless. So Radford turned his prone body and foot in the same direction as Yssaf's twist. The Berber hissed something under his breath and let go his useless hold.

But because of his bodily turn, Radford was now almost flat on his stomach. He could not see Yssaf clearly. He had to take a chance on what the Berber would do. He kicked out blindly. And he knew he had guessed correctly when he felt the heel of his boot slam into the man's ribs. Yssaf had half risen to his feet and, leaning forward, had been about to plunge his knife into Radford's back. Instead, he gave a grunt of agony and his knife hand wavered uncertainly in the air. But not for long.

In a single compact movement, Radford had turned on to his haunches and was again facing Yssaf. And he jabbed with his blade. He jabbed as a boxer might throw an in-fighting punch — short-travelling and with the roll of his shoulder behind it. But Yssaf's reflexes were fast, too. He jerked himself back and aside. Radford felt his knife tear and rip into the thick mass of robe gathered round Yssaf's waist. He tried to wrench it free. He could not do so. Some of the material had hooked itself over the shield at the bottom of the haft. His weapon was firmly locked in the Berber's clothing.

Yssaf snarled. It was a snarl of pure triumph. He gathered himself for the death lunge.

Radford forgot his own useless knife. He did the only thing possible — the classic emergency move in close combat. He attacked his enemy's weapon. He went straight and hard for Yssaf's knife, seeking to get his own hands round the hilt of it, too. When that happens, a man holding a knife wants automatically to jerk it away. It is another instinctive reaction. Yssaf did exactly that. It was his first serious mistake.

For something weird was happening to Radford's right hand . . .

Even while travelling at enormous speed, it changed course and bunched into a solid fist. That fist came down like a hammer. But not on any part of Yssaf's face or head. It crashed on to the inside of his bent elbow joint. The inside elbow is a sensitive part of the human frame. A main artery as well as nerve channels run through it, all of them near the surface. The effect on Yssaf was inevitable. He gave a choking gasp and his tongue fell forward from his open mouth. Then, after the first spasm of acute pain, his entire arm became numb, powerless.

The knife fell from his fingers.

But it did not reach the ground. Radford had hold of it before that could happen. And in the same second, he had pushed Yssaf so that the Berber was lying flat with Radford kneeling over him.

Radford pushed one hand under Yssaf's chin, forcing his head back. Then he placed the needle-sharp point of the blade against the front of the exposed neck. He pressed very slightly. Just hard enough to draw a faint trickle of blood.

He whispered in the Berber's ear: 'I can kill you any moment I choose! Even if your men shoot me, I'll be able to drive this into you before I die! But I don't want to kill you, Yssaf. I may not be your friend, but neither am I your enemy. I can prove that, if you'll listen to me. Will you listen, if I spare your life?'

Yssaf's voice replied in a strangled croak. 'Kill me, for I shall not make any pact with white vermin! I have lost our fight and my people will keep the pledge. You and your two friends will be allowed to leave this place unharmed.'

'You have courage,' Radford said. 'But I always knew that. You Berbers are a brave people. But is it that you, Yssaf, are not quite brave enough to hear the truth?'

It was a shrewd statement and question, which struck home. A little of the hatred went out of Yssaf's eyes. 'I do not plead for my life,' he said.

'You are not expected to plead — I know you would never do that, and neither would I. I want you to hear the truth about those who have been taken into slavery, for the Legion is not to blame. Those responsible for the crime were men disguised in the uniforms of legionnaires. And I want you to know of the evil being planned close to here in the deep ravine. It is an evil which will strike

174

at tens of thousands of your people this very night! Yssaf, if you are indeed loyal to the North African races, you will listen to me!'

Yssaf did not answer immediately. He remained completely still and seemingly unaware of the knife at his throat. Then he said: 'You have shown me that you fight like a man, Captain. So perhaps it is that you also speak as a man. Yes, I will hear you.'

Radford took the knife away. Putting out a hand, he helped Yssaf to his feet.

The other Berbers were gathering round. So were Peter and Professor Tiere, both wearing expressions of confused wonder, and annoyance that they did not understand the Berber tongue. Radford had just finished explaining to them when Yssaf said: 'All of us will sit under the rocks. There you will talk to me.'

★ ★ ★

Night had fallen and the story was told.

The three whites and a dozen Berbers sat huddled just within the entrance to the shallow cave. A crescent moon cast a pale, sickly light over them. Some way off, a fennec — the long-eared wild dog of the desert — howled as it hunted lizards.

Yssaf was asking questions. Radford found most of them difficult to answer clearly, for everything came back to the rockets and nuclear radiation. Yssaf was no fool, but at first he found it impossible to grasp even the basic facts. But eventually he and the other Berbers understood Radford's point that masses of people would die if the 'huge guns' were fired that night. He also understood the claim that enemies of France had enslaved the people of Gacruss to work in the ravine.

He perceived — but did he believe?

Yssaf said to Radford: 'We have heard you and you have spoken of things which are strange to our ears. Now I must talk with my warriors about your message.'

The Berbers withdrew a little way from Radford, Peter and Tiere. There they held a conference among themselves. Several times Radford looked anxiously towards them, then at his watch.

Once the professor said: 'You have me very puzzled, Hugh. Even if these Berbers agree to help, what can be done to stop the rockets? *Sacré!* You cannot think that a dozen tribesmen will be able to assault all those soldiers!'

'I certainly don't think anything of the sort,' Radford said. 'I have a different idea. It's a long shot and it means running awful risks because, if anything goes wrong the rockets might . . . ' He broke off, doubtful whether to continue.

Peter said: 'Let's hear the plan. You've got me kind of interested.'

'I think I'd better wait till the Berbers have made their decision,' Radford told him. 'If they're going to be our allies, they'll have to be treated as equals. That means we must all discuss our ideas together — and at the same time.'

At that moment Yssaf returned. He touched the centre of his forehead in a brief salute.

'Have you decided?' Radford asked him, hardly able to keep the anxiety out of his voice.

'Yes, we have decided, and it is the

judgment of all of us.'

'And what is it?'

'We do not believe all that you have told us.'

'Oh . . . you don't.'

'But neither do we disbelieve you. How can it be otherwise when we have no testimony save the sound of your voice? Can a blind man look into the distance and say that a friend approaches? The blind cannot do that and neither can we say that you speak the truth — or that you lie.'

'So you refuse to help? You won't try to save your peoples?'

Yssaf remained perfectly still for a short time. Then he shook his head slowly. 'We will help. Our muskets and our swords are yours to command. It cannot be otherwise, for if you speak truly, a terrible blight will fall on this land. But if you have lied to us, if you seek to ensnare us, a hideous death will strike at you!'

Radford gripped Yssaf's hand. 'You will soon know that I have not lied,' he said. 'Now listen to me, for we have so little time . . . '

As he spoke, he glanced again at his watch. It showed a few minutes after seven-thirty. In less than two and a half hours, the missiles were due to take off.

9

The Call of Yssaf

At the south end of the ravine, human misery was condensed. In that place the Arab slaves were resting. Stupefied, afraid and cowed, they lay on the hard ground. They had no covering against the cold of the night, save that provided by their work-tattered robes. A few slept fitfully, and when they stirred they groaned. Most were awake, staring silently at the slit of dark sky which showed above the tall walls of their prison.

Two burly sentries, each muffled in a greatcoat and each armed with an FN automatic rifle, stood guard over them. Although it was against standing orders, they sometimes talked to each other in whispers. And they continually checked the time. They felt an ever-increasing tension as the critical hour approached.

Far above them, at the top of the

ravine, another sentry was at his post. His nerves were strained, too. He was thinking of the moment when the great missiles would roar from their ramps to open a raw wound in the body of western civilisation. But this soldier could not find relief in snatched conversation. He stood alone. He guarded the pathway which led into the ravine.

He had done this duty often enough before and he had not minded it. Up to now, he had always found the isolation almost pleasant after close contact with his comrades. A man could walk about and listen to the howl of fennec or the squawk of vultures. He could sing softly to himself without disturbing anyone. And he could dream of the time — now so near — when the operation would be over and aircraft would land to take them all back to their far-distant homes.

But tonight the solitary sentry did not want to listen for animal sounds. Neither did he wish to sing. Nor even to walk along the edge of the ravine. The tension of time had stretched his nerves until they were like over-taut violin strings. He felt that they were going to snap at any moment. Tonight he hated his isolation. He wanted only to stand over the top of the rock-strewn pathway and stare down into the abyss where, under the great arc lamps, he could see men who looked as small as ants. And tents, and rockets, and the launching ramp all as small as toys. He craved to be down there tonight, among the warm company of his fellow men. Still, he told himself, he would not have so long to wait. Soon the guard would be changed. Soon his relief would arrive. Then he would be able to climb down that steep path, leaving the new sentry in this awful place.

What was that?

What had he heard?

It seemed very close to him. Just as if a man had pulled in a breath before speaking. But it couldn't be a man. He was the only man up here. Perhaps it was more like a gust of wind in the rocks. Yes, that was it. It must have been the wind.

But the wind had dropped some time ago. Now the air was quite calm. So what was it? Nothing, of course. Nothing at all.

Just nerves. No soldier should be expected to stand guard alone in such a place as this. Particularly on such a night as this.

There it was again . . .

But it was different this time. Not like a breath at all. Or like the vanished wind. Maybe it was his nerves again? No, it was not nerves. He had *heard* it. The faintest and the weirdest of sounds.

A bird or a desert dog? But they did not venture near humans.

Something small and hot was twisting in the depths of his stomach. And the muscles had drawn themselves into a tight ball. That must be because he was afraid. Yet he had never been afraid like this before! But always, until now, he had been able to see.

All this time he had been standing with his face to the ravine. And with his back to that sound. It must be because he feared to move.

Fear was paralysing him. That was not worthy of a soldier of the New Order. It was weakness and must be mastered.

Sweat was thick on the palms of his hands as he unslung his Lebel and turned.

In the moonlight there was nothing to be seen. But that cluster of nearby rocks might hide something. He cocked the rifle, then eased slowly forward.

'*Ah* . . . '

Something thin and strong had been dropped over his head. It was being drawn tight round his throat, choking him. He felt the rifle being lifted from his hands.

He was dying. He could not breathe . . .

★   ★   ★

Radford slackened the length of Berber sash cord. He put an arm round the sentry's waist and lowered him gently to the ground. Peter and Tiere appeared from behind the rocks. They were followed by Yssaf and his warriors.

Peter looked thoughtfully down at the inert figure. 'Is he dead?'

'No. We'll gag him and truss him up, then he won't be able to do us any harm.'

'That sure was something, the way you came up behind that guy when he turned around,' Peter said. 'How did you learn to move like that?'

'British commando training. It's one of the tricks of our trade. But it looks as if we're all going to have to use a lot more tricks before long. And there's one worry weighing heavily on my mind.'

'Tell me about it,' Peter said.

'I'm wondering when they're due to change the guard. If it's not for an hour, we have a chance. If it's any less, we've had our chips, and that goes for a lot of other people, too. We'll have to move fast.'

Radford gave an order to Yssaf. The Berber passed it on to one of his men, who proceeded to tie up the sentry. When that was done, Radford said: 'Lay him behind one of the rocks.' The warrior dragged the soldier away, then dropped him none too gently in a place of concealment.

A very noticeable change had come over the Berbers. Much of their suspicion had vanished. It was almost as if these natural warriors were beginning to enjoy themselves.

Radford gestured for them to gather round him. He told them: 'So far, it has been easy. Now we must be very careful. We have to get into the ravine without being heard or seen.'

Yssaf said with a touch of arrogance: 'We also can move as silently as birds on the wing. We shall follow you and no sound shall come from us.'

Radford realised that Yssaf's boast was probably true. But Peter and Professor Tiere were a different matter. It was not likely that either of them would be able to make the descent quietly. Particularly the elderly Tiere. But it was vital to have the professor with them. And the idea of leaving Peter behind was unthinkable. Anyway, the American would certainly refuse any order to remain out of the way.

Radford turned to his two friends. 'Moving down that path's going to be difficult,' he said. 'Particularly since we won't be able to see much. And remember what Balazki told us about their having to fix a rope ladder over a gap about halfway down? Be extra careful there. I'll lead, Yssaf and his men will follow me, and you two will bring up the rear. Whatever you do, don't try to hurry. If you're in trouble, take your time. If anyone makes a noise, we'll have failed before we're properly started.'

Peter shuffled awkwardly. He muttered something under his breath.

'What's on your mind?' Radford asked him.

'I'm a United States citizen.'

'That's hardly news to me, old chap. But why tell me about it now?'

'Because we Americans just don't bring up the tail end of any international queue. I figure my place is right in front, with you!'

This called for diplomacy. Radford understood Peter's feelings. But stealthy silence was not one of his virtues. It would be madness to let him take the lead.

'You've got to think of Professor Tiere,' Radford told him. 'The professor's not so young. He'll need one of us with him to give him some help — won't you, Professor?'

Tiere understood well enough. He nodded emphatically. Peter gave a reluctant shrug. 'Okay, he said. 'Maybe you're right.'

Radford handed the sentry's Lebel and ammunition pouches to Peter. 'Take charge of this. Put the pouches on and sling the rifle tightly over your back until we get to the bottom.' He moved to the edge of the ravine and looked at the rocky slope which led down to the ribbon of light and the midget figures far beneath. 'Let's go,' he said.

It was easy at first. They had the light from the moon and it showed the way fairly clearly. Here the path was, in fact, a series of large steps formed by the fall of rocks. They wound like a corkscrew, taking them in turn from left to right and always downward. Sometimes it was possible to step comfortably from one rock to another. Occasionally they had to brace themselves for a minor jump.

Radford was about a quarter of the way down when the dim light gave way to utter blackness. It would remain like that until they came within the radiance of the arc lamps near the bottom — and that would bring a special problem.

Completely unable to see, Radford hissed a warning to Yssaf, who was on the rock directly above. Then he probed cautiously with one foot. He located the edge of the stone and sat on it, legs dangling. Then, supporting himself with his hands, Radford lowered himself gently. His boots touched something which seemed solid enough. He put down his entire weight.

There was a harsh mechanical sound. A searing pain enveloped Red's legs. At the same time, something gripped them. Something of fantastic strength, for he could not shift them an inch in any direction. He gave a partly suppressed groan.

He panted to Yssaf: 'Something's holding my legs . . . I'm helpless . . . can't move!'

Radford sensed that Yssaf was leaning over him. He must have heard, but there was no reply. Abruptly, Radford knew the reason. In his torment, he had spoken in English. He repeated the agonised message, this time using the Berber dialect.

It was then that Yssaf showed that he had a clear mind. His first action was to warn the man directly behind him to stay where he was and to pass the order back. Having brought the entire descending column to a stop, Yssaf groped forward and touched Radford's shoulders.

'I will not try to pull you up,' he said. 'That might injure you. Before I can help, I must have light that I may see.'

Light! To show even a pin-point of it

was a risk. But not quite such a great risk as might at first be thought, for the arc lamps would tend to dazzle anyone in the ravine who chanced to look up.

Clenching his teeth against the pain, Red groped in a tunic pocket for his petrol lighter. Carefully shielding it with his body, he flicked the wheel. The wick broke into a tiny flame. But it was enough.

A pair of long steel bars were gripping his legs just below the knees, steel bars with serrated edges like teeth. They were hinged to a heavy metal base.

It was a man-trap, a trap of the type still used in parts of Europe to catch trespassers. But most enlightened countries had had them made illegal, for they could cost a victim his limbs, and sometimes even his life.

Yssaf lowered himself beside Radford. He stared with anxious curiosity at the vicious mechanism. Obviously, he had never before seen anything remotely like it. He took hold of the notched bars and tried to force them apart.

'You'll never manage it,' Radford told him. 'When I stood on this I released a high-tension spring. The only . . . only hope is to get some leverage. Try using your musket.'

Yssaf thrust his musket between the retaining rods and pulled. All his strength was needed, but the teeth parted. With a grunt of relief, Radford dragged his legs clear. Almost immediately the pain lessened. There were deep cuts in his leather leggings but they had protected him from injury. He and Yssaf dragged the trap aside.

Radford realised that they now faced a new and completely unexpected danger. It was probable that other traps lay open on the path into the ravine. They must have been placed there as an extra discouragement to the Arab slaves who might think of trying to escape. To attempt to continue the descent in total darkness would be asking for disaster. Radford knew that he must from now on have some light, however faint, to guide him.

His petrol lighter was the only answer. But it must be used very carefully.

He explained to Yssaf what he was going to do. 'I'll flick it on for just a second before I move onto each new rock,' he said. 'I'll try to cover it with my hands and body, so that it can't be seen from the bottom. Don't try to follow me until I say that it's safe.'

To Radford's surprise, Yssaf put out an inquisitive land. 'Let me see your strange beacon,' he said. 'How can it make fire so easily?'

'Not now,' Radford said. 'But I promise you, Yssaf, if we get through this night alive, I'll present it to you.'

By now, the other Berbers were whispering curiously, not knowing the reason for the delay. Far to the rear and therefore still having the advantage of some moonlight, Peter and Professor Tiere must be wondering, too. Although his legs were still painful, Radford decided to move on without more delay, so as to prevent any indiscreetly shouted inquiry.

Using the petrol lighter had one advantage — it made progress faster than it would otherwise have been. And at Radford's suggestion, the whole column closed up so that each man could whisper information on what lay ahead to the one behind him.

Radford found another man-trap. Jaws open, as if waiting hungrily for a victim, it stood directly under the edge of a tall rock. Anyone trying to escape up the path would probably kneel on it, so that the teeth closed on his body. Radford sprang it, then pushed it out of harm's way.

Halfway, they came to a short stretch of flat ground. At the end of it he saw the rope ladder. It was secured to a pair of steel stanchions driven into the edge of a drop. But how deep was that drop? Radford could not use his lighter to discover that without running an exceptional risk of its being seen. But it was best for all to know how far they were to climb down through the complete blackness. There was a quick and safe way of finding out — he pulled the ladder up. Its length was about thirty feet, the height of an average house. Under these conditions, that was too much for comfort. Particularly since rope ladders tended to sway like pendulums when anyone was moving up or down them.

Radford passed the information back. Then he returned the ladder over the ledge after counting the rungs. There were twenty-seven of them.

That part of the descent was a little easier than he had expected because the rough rock face checked some of the natural rope sway. When his feet were on the twenty-fifth rung, Radford stopped. Holding the lighter close to his chest, he peered down. No trap there. The ground immediately below was safe.

He held the bottom of the ladder steady while Yssaf came down. Then he moved on. It soon became clear that the last half was to be much less difficult. The pathway sloped less acutely and the rocks were smaller. It came almost as a surprise to Radford when he realised that he no longer needed to use his lighter. The reflected glow from the arc lamps was there. Now they would have to be even more careful. But all of them knew the drill.

Radford crouched nearly double. As the others came into the area of illumination, they did the same.

The lamps, connected by heavy armoured cable, were secured into the rock face about twenty feet from the bottom. Saucer-shaped reflectors directed their beam down.

As Red came level with them, he dropped to his hands and knees. Then he paused to make a careful survey.

Arabs were below him. The Arabs of Gacruss. Almost a hundred and fifty of them, men and women, young and old. Radford looked at them anxiously. All were stretched full length and at least some were sleeping. They were thin, worn-looking. That was only to be expected after long days of forced labour on a minimum of food. But there was something else. Something much more important. It could not be seen — only sensed. Yet it was unmistakable. It was an atmosphere of surrender — of complete resignation to an unjust fate. It lay heavily upon those Arabs, as dark and as forbidding as a shroud.

It was as if the last faint spark of fight had faded from the hearts of the people of Gacruss. Yet somehow that spark must be rekindled.

Radford turned his attention to the sentries — two of them. They were standing just beyond the outer fringe of Arabs. They were talking, FN automatic rifles slung over their shoulders. Beyond them there was a clear hundred yards of empty ravine before one came to the first of the tents. And those appeared to be supply tents, for no one was near them.

But from the centre of the ravine onwards, there was plenty of activity. Particularly round the launching ramp, and the massive rocket upon it. There a cluster of civilian technicians were making final checks. Some of them were gathered in front of what seemed to be an electronic computer. A short distance from the ramp, a smaller group of civilians were talking. Radford could not be sure, but he thought he recognised Dr. Goerler among them, leaning on his stick.

The three other rockets lay on the huge articulated wagon, ready for transfer in their turn to the ramp. Soldiers were bustling round them.

Radford could almost imagine a name written on each of those nuclear missiles. Names spelt in letters of blood. *Casablanca, Oran, Algiers, Tunis* . . .

Yssaf had arrived at his side. The Berber's gaze was directed only at the sentries. His dark eyes were glittering with the pleased anticipation which Radford had seen once before.

'This will be easy,' Yssaf whispered. 'Those two chatter together like a pair of old women. They expect no trouble.'

Radford did not feel quite so confident, but he did not say so. He glanced behind and could just make out the unmoving heads of some of the tribesmen as they crouched as still as corpses. Then he said to Yssaf: 'If we use the cover of the rocks, we can get fairly close to them without being seen. But we can't rush them — there's too much clear ground to cover. When we're as near as possible, we'll have to lure them to us as we did with the soldier at the top.'

Yssaf nodded. He put his musket on the ground and drew out his short knife. He tested the edges of it against the black hairs of his beard.

Radford took out the Luger and checked that the safety catch was on. He did not want to use it as a gun. With silence the first necessity, it would have to serve as a cudgel. Its long, round barrel made it almost ideal for that purpose, giving a good grip. The heavy butt could deliver a lethal blow.

Leaving the others, they began crawling nearer to the sentries. Their main difficulty was to avoid dislodging the many loose stones. And Radford found the rough surface particularly painful to his still-throbbing leg.

But progress had to be slow and careful, for they were now under intense light. This was particularly so at one point, where the rocks were so low that they had to wriggle on their stomachs to avoid being seen.

It took them fully ten minutes to cover the twenty feet to the bottom of the ravine. There they took cover behind a boulder and paused to catch their breath. Radford took a swift peep at the sentries. They were about fifteen paces away and still talking. He heard snatches of their conversation, but it meant nothing to him, not being able to understand the language.

A sudden recollection made Radford look at his wristwatch. He gave a very faint sigh of uneasiness. It was twenty-eight minutes past nine!

Now only thirty-two minutes left before the first missile was due to be fired! Thirty-two minutes in which to achieve the next to impossible.

Radford gave a nod to Yssaf. The Berber made a brief gesture with his knife as a reply. He was ready.

Radford pursed his lips. Through them he produced a short, faint and nondescript sort of sound. It could have been made by an animal, a man, or even by the wind.

But the two sentries went on talking without pause. They had not heard it.

Radford tried again — this time just a little louder and holding the peculiar note a second longer.

Suddenly the sentries were quiet. Then one of them spoke in low tones. The other answered with a single word. Silence again. They must be listening.

Radford raised the butt of the Luger. With it, he tapped twice on the boulder. A large bird might have made such a noise while foraging with its beak. It was no more than a slight disturbance, calculated to arouse curiosity but not alarm.

Boots crunched. They were coming towards the boulder. Radford's grip tightened on the barrel of the pistol. Yssaf balanced his knife in an open palm.

They could not see, so they had to judge distance by the sound of those steps alone. But a man's sense of hearing can give a lot of information beyond the obvious when he knows how to use it. To Radford and Yssaf, an important fact became clear. It was that the sentries had separated. Each intended to come round a different side of the stone. It could hardly be better.

Radford slightly eased his position. He knew that Yssaf was doing the same.

The barrel and vented piston housing of an FN automatic rifle appeared round the angle of the boulder. Then a big man, clad in a Legion greatcoat. With his left hand, Radford went for the gun. He went for the trigger. And he had his thumb behind it, so that it could not be squeezed, while the sentry was in mid-stride. He pulled ferociously at the gun, at the same time jerking the soldier forward and down. He was too surprised to call out. And he never had time to recover from that surprise. For Radford's Luger crashed against the side of his skull. He uttered a whimpering moan. Then he folded to the ground as if every bone in his body had suddenly dissolved.

Radford looked round. Yssaf had been even quicker — and much less merciful. He was already wiping his blade clean and looking with satisfaction at the sentry who lay in front of him. A sentry who would never move again.

But already Radford's eyes were gazing beyond Yssaf to the northern part of the ravine. Everything seemed to be carrying on there as before. It seemed that no one had seen the disappearance of the two guards. There was a good chance that their absence would remain unnoticed for a long time, since the nearest men at the north end were more than a quarter of a mile away. And all were very busy.

Radford picked up one of the automatic rifles and got to his feet. By doing that, he lessened the danger of any alarm, for being in Legion uniform he would almost certainly be taken for one of the guards if anyone happened to look that way. He raised a hand in a signal. The Berbers, with Peter and the professor, sprang into view. Quickly, they slithered down the rest of the slope, then stood at the side of the ravine, close to the Arabs.

The Arabs . . .

All were awake now. A few were standing, but most were squatting on their haunches. Beyond that, they were showing no reaction. They were staring about them in dull apathy, as if their minds as well as their bodies were drained of all strength.

Radford and Yssaf joined the others. Peter said: 'Another smart piece of work, Hugh. Maybe you were — '

But Radford interrupted him. He had looked again at his watch. It showed twenty-seven minutes to ten. He said to Yssaf: 'Now you take over! Try to talk some life into those Arabs — and talk fast!'

Yssaf advanced into the middle of the huddle of slaves. They watched him, but indifferently. It seemed that nothing was capable of surprising even them anymore.

'We come to you as liberators,' Yssaf said, his firm voice carrying well. 'Have we not rid you of your guards? Yes, you are indeed free. Even the traps with teeth of iron have been taken from yonder pathway, and no sentry is at the top. Those among you who cannot fight may leave now. You can return to Gacruss!'

A few of them stirred slightly and one or two mumbled. But otherwise there was still no reaction.

Radford said to Peter: 'Yssaf's putting it over well, but it's like talking to a lot of people who are half-doped!'

Yssaf was continuing: 'You must know that you have been made to work on machines of death. They will bring death this very night to a multitude of our people — unless the young and the strong among you help us to destroy them!'

Again no response. The Arabs did not even seem to be fully listening. They were gazing into empty space now, rather than at Yssaf.

'We know how to prevent these machines going into the sky,' Yssaf went on. 'But we need you at our side — have none of you hearts brave enough to strike in defence of his own people?'

Yssaf let the question hang in the air. For a few moments it looked as if his efforts would again be useless. But there was a sudden movement at the back of the small crowd. An elderly Arab got to his feet. He was as thin as any of the others. His face was deeply lined with exhaustion as well as age. But he was by no means decrepit. He looked hard at Yssaf, who stared back.

'You are a Berber,' the Arab said, pronouncing the words with scorn.

'I am indeed a Berber, and I boast of it!'

'It was ever thus. You boast and you slay — that is known to us all. But now you become liars and traitors!'

The accusation came so suddenly, so unexpectedly, that Yssaf momentarily rocked under it. Then fury gripped him. He gripped his knife and began to move on the Arab.

Radford called: 'Stop! Leave him!'

Yssaf paused to transfer his glare to Radford. 'I shall kill him! You heard the words he used! No man speaks so of me and my race and lives to repeat it!'

'Let him explain,' Radford said. 'He

must have his reasons. Once we know them, we may also learn why they are all so indifferent about helping us.'

Yssaf hesitated, then fixed another glittering gaze on the Arab.

'You have heard what the white man said! Tell me why you charge us with being traitors and liars!'

The Arab folded his arms across his chest. He said: 'You come to us in the company of three white people, one of them an officer of the Legion, and you say that you are liberators! What trickery is this? Have not legionnaires brought us here and treated us as serfs? Is it not the French who have made the great missiles?'

Radford felt an urgent hammering of his heart. So they had indeed uncovered the reason for the indifference! It was twenty-four minutes to ten . . .

'Wait! Let me talk!' Shouting the words, Radford ran forward until he was standing beside Yssaf. Then he spoke quickly to all the Arabs.

'Those men who took you into this slavery were not legionnaires. They come from far across the sea to the north. They draped themselves as men of the Legion so that France would be condemned for all that they did — and intend to do this night! You remember Taiba, the aged headman of your village? Taiba was left by these enemies, for they thought he would perish. But he reached Fort Allengrah and told of all that had happened.'

There was an abrupt gabble of many voices. And at the mention of Taiba, most of the Arabs stood up.

Radford went on: 'The government of France was angered that such a crime should be committed. I was sent to Fort Allengrah to talk with Taiba. But that I could not do. For Fort Allengrah was destroyed by these same evil ones who make slaves of you! Taiba died in that fort. But he was not alone. All the legionnaires there died with him. The blood of your headman mingled with the blood of France!'

All the Arabs were standing now. All were watching Radford with eyes which were transfixed. The last remnant of lassitude had gone.

But their spokesman was not yet convinced. He remained motionless, arms still folded. 'You speak with a clever tongue,' he said. 'But why should we believe this? How can we know it is not one more trap?'

Radford hesitated for only a moment. His brain was working at lightning speed. 'Fort Allengrah was destroyed by rockets fired when the sun was high two days ago,' he said. 'You must have seen those rockets fired from here! And on this very day yet another rocket was fired on the French and their friends who visited the ruins of the fort. I and the two white people with me escaped, but all the others perished. That rocket, also, you must have seen. You saw it because you were here. But how could I know of it unless I speak the truth, for till a few hours ago I was never in this ravine!'

There was another gabble of excited voices, louder and more prolonged this time. But Radford quietened them.

'You saw a strange plane come down here today,' he shouted. 'We were in it! Yes, we were searching for the evil ones when we were captured by them. We escaped, yet our plane was destroyed. Are you blind that you did not see our plane burn on the edge of the cliff? Did your eyes not see their guns sweep this ravine?'

The Arab spokesman unfolded his arms. Almost all hostility had gone from him. 'We saw that indeed,' he said. 'But how does it come that you are now with these Berbers?'

'Because when the Berbers heard our story, they in their courage and wisdom offered their lives and their swords to save their fellow men! They believe that you will have spirit enough to do the same!'

The elderly Arab walked towards Radford. He gave a brief salaam.

'Your words are truly spoken,' he said. 'There are wonders here that we do not understand, but we know that death is plotted for a multitude. We, the people of Gacruss, like to live in peace. But we are no less men than warrior tribes such as the Berbers. So I say we shall fight with you. We have no weapons save our hands, but even with those we can slay!'

There was a murmur of approval from the Arabs. Now they were eager, expectant. They were gathering close round Radford, their eyes never leaving him.

Radford told them: 'We must strike with cunning, for I do not want any of you to die needlessly. We have a plan and all of you must obey it. Let all of you do as I shall direct and let none hesitate, for there is so little time left. First, we . . . '

Yssaf was touching his shoulder. Red looked at him, then followed the Berber's intent gaze.

Four soldiers were approaching. They were marching stiffly and precisely. They were still a long way off, and it seemed they had noticed nothing to alarm them. Not yet. But they soon would.

Radford's earlier fear had become reality.

This must be the new guard. The sentries were about to be changed.

10

Battleground

Peter pushed urgently through the crowd towards Radford. He was holding the other FN rifle. He patted the butt. 'I'm a good shot. I figure I can pick those guys off before they get close enough to make trouble.'

Radford shook his head. 'Thanks for the offer, but I don't think much of it. If we fire just a single shot, it'll raise the whole ravine. Remember how sounds echo here. We'll have to fix it so they march right up to us.'

'That sounds just fine, but how can we get them to do that? Those boys aren't nuts! They'll soon see the sentries aren't here!'

'I'm thinking that you and I can look like the sentries.'

'Say, do you figure they're marching this way with their eyes shut? They'll see the difference. You're in Legion uniform okay, but you're an officer and that makes you look different! Your cap's different. So are those leather leggings of yours. You'd never pass for a buck private and you know it!'

'I'm going to use one of the caps worn by the guards that Yssaf and I have just fixed. That ought to make the top bit of me look all right. You'll put on the other one, Peter. We'll stand right in the middle of these Arabs, as if we're settling some small squabble. Only our heads will show. Got it?'

'Yeah, maybe . . . '

'Then fetch the caps — and move fast!'

Peter rushed towards the boulder where the guard lay hidden from view. When he returned with the two *kepis*, Radford had finished giving quick, brief order to the Arabs. They understood. Then he turned to Yssaf.

'The rest will be for you and your men. Let there be no sound, no disturbance!'

'It will be thus,' Yssaf said.

Peter put on a *kepi*. It was several sizes too small and he had to force it over his head. Radford's was a slightly better fit. They slung the automatic rifle over their shoulders while the Arabs packed closely round them. The Berbers took up positions on the outer fringe of the crush, nearest the approaching soldiers. They had hidden their muskets, and their knives were up the sleeves of their robes. Those Berber robes were in much better condition than those worn by the Arabs of Gacruss. But, mingling with so many, the difference was not likely to be noticed immediately.

Radford looked over the top of the crowd. The soldiers were now less than four hundred yards away. One of them was wearing the stripes of a senior N.C.O. They were marching quickly. But Radford knew that they could not be too quick. For his watch showed thirteen minutes to ten.

Then he noticed Professor Tiere. The little Frenchman was among the Arabs and some way off. Because he was so short, his bare head and western suit would probably not be seen. But Radford was not prepared to take that chance.

'Professor — sit on the ground,' he

said. The professor made a Gallic gesture and obeyed, becoming completely invisible.

Radford shifted his position so that his back was to the approaching guards. He told Peter to do the same. Then he gave a sign to the Arabs. They all began to talk at the same time. Some of them pushed each other, as if tempers were running high. Several, facing the length of the ravine, made imploring gestures to Radford and Peter, as men would when appealing for justice.

Two hundred yards away, the sergeant gave a word of command. The new guard halted. The sergeant peered forward with puzzled concern. He could see the backs of the heads of the two men on duty, but that was all. They were surrounded by a sea of Arabs. He would soon put a stop to this.

He rapped out another command. He and his three men broke into a trot, at the same time unslinging their rifles. Two were armed with FNs, two with Lebels.

He got to within a dozen yards of the outer fringe of Arabs. Then he again called a halt. He roared a few blistering words of warning at the heaving throng. They had no effect — none at all. The noise went on as before.

The sergeant decided that a warning shot was needed. Just one round fired over their head. That ought to be enough. If it was not, he would put a volley into the middle of them. That would not matter, for their work was done.

But some of the Arabs on the outside of the crowd were falling back. It looked as if they wanted no part in the trouble and were seeking the protection of the guards. They were moving round the sides of his three men. They —

It was at that moment that the N.C.O. realised that they were not ordinary Arabs. Their robes were different. They were tall, strong. In their eyes there were lights of black, fanatical hatred. Their lips were pulled back in smiles of satanic fury.

They were looking at him! Looking at him and his men. Surrounding the four of them. And, as if by witchcraft, knives had appeared in their hands. Horrible, barbarous knives. There would be no time. No time even to fire one round. The knives were flashing towards them . . .

★   ★   ★

Dr. Goerler closed the inspection hatch at the base of the missile. He came down the steps from the ramp and looked upwards at the vast, tapering shape. It was complete now. Absolutely complete. An hour before, the nuclear warhead had been locked in the nose. Directly behind the warhead was the radar-electronic circuit which, once optimum height had been reached in the stratosphere, would guide the last stage of the missile towards Casablanca. Any small errors which might develop could be detected and rectified by radio signals transmitted from this ravine.

Goerler hooked his stick over an arm and rubbed his hands with satisfaction. Then he looked at the three other waiting rockets. They, too, were ready. Their circuits had been fixed for their various targets. All that remained was to load them on the ramp as their turn came and connect the bases to a single thin wire.

It was all most satisfactory. He would surely be commended for this when he returned to his homeland. Perhaps he would even be congratulated by the Leader himself . . .

Goerler came out of his brief daydream as he saw Balazki approaching. Balazki, too, looked content.

'Nine minutes left, Doctor,' he said. 'Nine minutes, then the first of our toys rises into space. And forty-five minutes from now will see our work completed. There have been hitches,' he went on reflectively, 'but we have overcome them. We can be satisfied. But I admit I was worried this afternoon. Those three fools might easily have wrecked this ramp. I blame myself, for I should have had them shot as soon as they landed here.'

A sudden thought occurred to Goerler. 'They may be watching us now,' he piped.

'Let them. They can do us no harm. Tomorrow, before we are flown home, I will send out a search party to bring them in. We might as well take them with us. Our government will be most interested to meet them, particularly the professor.

And I have been thinking about that English-man. He is supposed to be a Legion officer and his papers bear that out, but I have a feeling he is something more than that. His mind is quick and original. I almost have a respect for him. He is most unlike an ordinary army officer.'

Goerler was not particularly interested. He glanced towards the main control tent. There his assistants were waiting in front of the main computer. Another was seated before a small switch. And he kept glancing at a chronometer. Thirty seconds from take-off time, that man would begin his countdown. At exactly ten o'clock he would throw the switch.

Goerler said: 'There'll be a great deal of noise when the rockets rise. Much more than we had when we fired the small one.'

'Of course,' Balazki said with a trace of impatience. 'I'm well aware of that.'

'I'm thinking of the Arabs,' Goerler piped on. 'They might panic and cause trouble. That could be awkward, since nearly all our soldiers will be busy on the loading wagon.'

Balazki said: 'It's part of my job to

think of such things. Normally the guard is changed at this time. But I have given orders for the old guard to remain for the time being with the new one. The extra men will be quite enough to subdue any fright among the Arabs. They will shoot a few of them if necessary,' he added casually.

As he finished speaking, Balazki glanced automatically towards the south end of the ravine. He expected to see a faint, indefinite smudge there. A sort of haze of distant material which marked the place where the Arabs were concentrated.

There was no smudge. No haze.

He twitched his hard eyes and looked again, wondering whether the long distance and the fierce artificial light were playing tricks with his vision.

His vision was all right. The far end of the ravine was empty of life!

He jerked a pair of field-glasses from their case. Adjusting the focus wheel, he stared through them. Now he could see the place in clear detail. Not a trace of the Arabs! Nor of their guards!

But wait . . . Something was happening

at the side of the ravine, on that pathway which led out of the place. People were climbing up there. Most of them climbing slowly and with difficulty. He could make out the details of those at the rear end, who were still within the beams of the arc lamps. They were the old men with women and children. They were escaping, and no one was stopping them!

But where were the young men among the Arabs? And where were the soldiers?

There was movement against the sheer cliff walls, fast but stealthy and partly hidden by the supply tents. They were Arabs, advancing towards them in two columns. The column on the left was being led by a familiar uniformed figure. It was Captain Radford! And the American was leading at the other side! Many of them seemed to be armed.

A flow of pure panic rippled through Balazki's body. He could handle any emergency which he understood. But this was beyond all reason. Already, the two columns were well over halfway towards the ramp. And his soldiers — his magnificently trained and carefully chosen soldiers

— they were working round the missiles' transport equipment, their rifles and ammunition pouches stacked in their billets.

Balazki screamed a warning. At the same time, he ran towards the administrative tent.

'Sound the alarm siren! Sound it!'

But for precious seconds, the men there only gazed at him, their faces slack with amazement.

'We're being attacked!'

At last, someone rushed to the switch which controlled the siren.

★   ★   ★

Radford saw Balazki's rush. Faintly, he heard him shout. The time for caution was over. This was the vital moment — the moment when they must strike as hard and as fast as an army in the field. In the first phase, everything depended on preventing Balazki's soldiers getting to their rifles. He called across to the other side of the ravine: 'This is it, Peter! Go to it!'

The American's voice came back: 'I'm almost there!'

The two columns broke away from the sides of the ravine. They charged. At the same time, they formed themselves into a ragged V-shaped formation, the armed men at each apex, the people of Gacruss following. Radford had Yssaf with him, and half of the Berbers. Yssaf was gripping an FN and his knife was between his teeth. Tiere was in Peter's column, with the rest of the Berbers. The professor had armed himself with a Lebel, which he seemed to know how to use.

Already, although several hundred yards divided them from their enemy, the Berbers were breaking into a hideous battle cry. Radford hoped none of them would open fire too soon. Ammunition was precious.

Suddenly the howling of the Berbers was drowned by the alarm siren, the high-pitched whine which they had heard before.

The result was instantaneous. Soldiers who had been working, stripped to the waist, broke away from the missiles. They ran towards their billet tents.

The range was much longer than

Radford liked. But he could not wait. Holding his FN against his hip, he squeezed the trigger and held it back momentarily. Eight of the twenty rounds in the box magazine sprayed out. They cut between the soldiers and their tents. Three men ran into the squirt of lead. They jumped into the air, convulsed, then lay still where they fell.

Now the three others with FNs were opening fire. And the range was rapidly getting shorter. Their aim was not accurate — understandably, since they were running. But several of the bullets ripped among the stunned soldiers, and many of them fell.

The soldiers could not be blamed for their bewilderment or for succumbing to panic. They had been taken utterly by surprise. They were under fire from a charging mob. And they were unarmed with no chance of reaching the rifles which were in the billet tents..

For a few seconds, the soldiers of the Black Legion huddled together, making a perfect target. Then when more of them fell, they broke and ran. Some clawed for useless concealment behind the girders of the ramp. Others ran to the transports. A few flung up their hands, hoping for mercy.

Now it was as if a floodgate had broken. Or as though the bars of a great cage had opened, releasing ferocious and avenging hounds.

The V-formation ceased to exist among the attackers because the unarmed Arabs who had been at the rear had drawn level with the others. In wild fury, the people of Gacruss rushed towards those who had enslaved and tormented them. They descended on cringing soldiers, seeking vengeance with their bare hands. In these moments, the people of Gacruss were just as ruthless as the Berbers.

By the vehicle park . . .

There seven soldiers had recovered some of their nerve. They had climbed into an open motor truck. With a shaking hand, one of them switched on the ignition and started the engine. He trod savagely on the throttle and the truck surged forward, seeking to plough through the screeching mob, seeking to reach the south end of the ravine and make an escape up that track.

They did not get more than ten yards. A wall of Arabs parted, as if to let them through. Then the wall closed in on them. Wild hands grabbed at them, dragging them from the truck. And the truck was turned onto its side.

At the back of the ramp . . .

Dr. Goerler was screaming in concentrated terror. He had tried to climb the girders and had reached a height of seven or eight feet. Now a couple of Berbers and a dozen Arabs were holding on to his ankles, his legs and parts of his clothing, all trying to wrench him down.

But terror had given him strength. Somehow he was holding on. His shoes were pulled from his feet, his jacket torn from his body. But he stayed there. One of the Berbers, a knife in his teeth, began climbing the girder towards him.

It would have been over in a few seconds.

But it was then that Peter saw what was happening. Using the strength of his enormous shoulders, he propelled himself through the horde. He reached the girder as the Berber was about to strike. The blade was poised over Goerler's neck. Peter gripped his FN rifle by the barrel and swung the butt upward. The wood slammed against the knife, knocking it out of the Berber's hand. The Berber stared down at Peter in thwarted fury, and there was a rumble of indignation from the others. But it faded abruptly, for it was then that Goerler fainted. He released his hold on the girder, slid a little way down it, then dropped at Peter's feet.

Peter picked him up easily, slinging him over or shoulder. 'You're not murdering him or anyone else if can help it!' he shouted. 'You guys can only kill where you come up against resistance!'

They did not understand his words. But his actions had a clear enough meaning. And, because the Berbers and Arabs already respected the American, they let him carry Goerler to a place of comparative safety.

In the control tent . . .

The computer and radar which were to guide the rockets took up most of the space — a long panel of dials and flickering lights. Four technical assistants sat in front of them, faces drawn and white as they heard the chaos outside. But they were not deserting their posts. They were dedicated to the task of sending off those missiles, and the time had all but arrived. For one of them, seated before a switch, had started the countdown.

' . . . twenty-eight . . . twenty-seven . . . twenty-six . . . '

He called the seconds in a low, flat voice. Nothing, this technician told himself, could prevent the first rocket taking off. If anyone should try to stop him before the count reached zero, he had only to press the switch under his hand. But he would much rather have the satisfaction of carrying out his orders exactly. A few seconds did not matter, but he had always been taught that blind obedience was the greatest virtue.

His eyes were fixed on the hand of a chronometer.

' . . . eighteen . . . seventeen . . . sixteen . . . '

He put his forefinger on the switch. A

firm pressure was all that was needed. Then a nuclear missile would rise from the ramp towards Casablanca. And it looked as if it would rise exactly on time. He did not know what was happening outside, but if anyone near the ramp were scorched to a cinder by the initial heat blast, that did not matter. All that mattered was to get the missile away.

' . . . twelve . . . eleven . . . ten . . . nine . . . '

A man burst into the tent. A small harmless-looking man in civilian clothes and pince-nez clipped to his nose.

But . . . But he was holding a rifle. It was on his shoulder, and he was sighting it.

The technician told himself: *Press the switch now!*

The message went from his brain to his nerves. But nothing happened. The finger seemed to be swaying in misty space. There was a hot agony in his arm and a crash of vicious sound in his ears.

In the moment before all became black, the technician realised that he had been shot by the harmless-looking man.

Now several Arabs had joined Tiere. But the professor did not notice them. He was standing over the switch and examining the wiring, tracing it back. Presently, Tiere found what he wanted at a place behind the computer panel. He took out his pocket knife and prised open a small plastic box. Out of the box he lifted a thin length of black carbonyl and a glass fuse case. He ground them under his feet. Then, exhausted, he leaned against the side of the tent. But he was smiling. For the missile firing leads were disconnected.

And Radford . . .

Balazki was his main concern. Until Balazki was accounted for, anything could happen. Radford saw him run into the administration tent. It was not easy to follow quickly because masses of struggling, shouting men kept blocking his way. But at last he pushed through the flap.

It was one of the largest tents — almost of marquee size. It contained several small desks, all littered with papers, plus a filing cabinet and typewriters. The handful of soldiers who worked there were standing in a scared huddle. They, too, had been unable to get to their rifles.

But Balazki was armed. He stood well apart from the others. He was gripping a pistol and it was aimed at the centre of Radford's stomach.

'So this is the end,' Balazki said. There was no trace of fear in his tones, no call for mercy.

'For once I agree with you,' Radford told him. 'For you and those who have worked with you, this looks like the finish.'

'Do you know why I came in here?' Balazki asked. 'I'll tell you — it was not to run away, it was to be sure that certain important documents were destroyed. That has been done, and — '

'Destroyed or not, documents will not make much difference now, Balazki. We have all the evidence we need against your country.'

Balazki gave a slow nod. Then he said: 'Before we go any further, I want to ask a question which interests me a great deal. Are you a genuine officer of the Legion?'

'I hold a Legion commission,' Red said with perfect truth, knowing that an emergency rank had been given him by the Defence Ministry.

'That does not take us far enough, Captain Radford. I, too, have held various ranks of convenience. But the simple fact is that your resourcefulness and your extraordinary nerve make me think that you may be . . . well, an international agent. I know well enough that such agents, no matter which country employs them, are very exceptional men. I'm bound to admit that you seem to have every qualification. Are you an agent, Captain Radford?'

Radford did not answer. Balazki gave a short, guttural laugh.

'Your silence answers my question,' he added. 'It is one more reason for killing you — and I'm going to kill you!'

Radford shifted his gaze to Balazki's pistol. And at the same time he realised that his own rifle was not aimed at Balazki. It was pointed in a general direction to cover the main group of soldiers in the tent. No matter how fast he moved, he obviously would not have time to swing it round before Balazki pulled his trigger.

'But why kill me?' Radford asked. 'It won't do you any good.'

'It will be a means of getting rid of a very dangerous enemy agent. And it will also give me a lot of satisfaction to know that I have evened a personal account with you. I will shoot you — then I shall kill myself!'

Balazki was not bluffing. He was speaking with quiet, lethal seriousness. Radford knew that, short of some miracle, his only chance was to try to talk the man out of using the gun.

'You'd be wiser to surrender to me, Balazki.'

'Give me one good reason why I should.'

'If you surrender, you'll at least receive a fair trial.'

'You must be joking, Captain Radford! Surely this is no time for humour! What justice can I expect, except that of being torn to pieces by your rabble of Arabs? In any case, I don't want to live. I have failed in my mission and for that I blame myself and you. That's a good enough reason to take your life as well as my own.'

'You'll not be touched by the Arabs, Balazki, even though you may deserve it. I have given strict orders that there's to be no senseless killing. It may be difficult to enforce that order — but it will be done. I give you my word on that.'

Balazki snorted. 'So you whine for your life!'

'I do not! But neither do I want to be shot by you, or anyone else. And I don't see why you should run away from justice!'

Balazki shook his head. 'I'm not running away. I'm moving forward to meet my fate. Now — now I'll pull the trigger . . . '

Radford saw Balazki's forefinger tighten. There was a swish of robes. And Radford glimpsed a tall figure throwing itself in front of him. In the same second, Balazki's pistol gave a spitting bark.

Yssaf's whole body shook, as if he had received a heavy punch. Then his knife swept through the air. It entered Balazki's chest, over the heart. Balazki was dead before he touched the ground.

And Yssaf . . .

The bullet had torn through both his lungs and it should have finished him immediately. But some men fight to the end. They do not easily surrender anything, least of all their lives. Yssaf was one such as they. He swayed and half-turned to Radford. Radford dropped his automatic rifle and caught him. Gently, he lowered the Berber into a camp chair.

When Yssaf spoke, each word was forced through a blanket of agony. He whispered: 'I am sorry your skin is white . . . we would have made mighty warriors together, you and I . . . '

Radford said softly: 'I could never be such a warrior as you, Yssaf my friend.'

'Yet you defeated me in the battle of the knives.' He smiled wanly, then added: 'I have gained . . . gained my reward, have I not?'

'Your reward . . . ?'

'The beacon. Had I let that man slay you, the beacon could never have been mine.'

Radford understood. He took the petrol lighter from his tunic pocket and pressed it into Yssaf's hand, Yssaf gazed at it proudly for a few moments, His fingers closed over it. Then, silently, he died.

Peter and Professor Tiere came into the tent. They watched as Radford covered Yssaf's face.

'How did it happen?' Peter asked.

'He died saving my life and to win a reward,' Red said. 'Yssaf wasn't like any of us, but he was a great man. I'll tell you about it later . . . Is the fighting over?'

'It is. But at first the Arabs and Berbers wanted to kill all Balazki's men.'

'You stopped them, I hope.'

'I managed it, but there's been some mighty rough treatment handed out. Anyway, all the prisoners are rounded up and there's no more danger from the rockets.'

With Peter and Tiere following him, Radford went outside. He did not want to look at the ghastly havoc around him. Instead, he stared up at the sky for a few seconds, watching the peaceful moon. Then he walked slowly to the radio tent.

Except for one Berber standing guard, the place was deserted. He sat himself before the powerful transmitter and adjusted the frequency levels before sending out a signal to Legion headquarters at Sidi bel Abbes.

'*Calling PKT . . . calling PKT . . .* '

As he waited for a reply, he looked at his watch. It was four minutes after ten.

And no vile missiles were hurtling through the sky. Nor would they ever do so from that ravine in the Sahara. The teeming multitudes of Casablanca were safe, not knowing of the horror which they had escaped by a fraction of a minute. In Oran, Algiers and Tunis, they would live, although death had been planned for them.

No cause now for Africa to be set aflame, no cause for massacre, no reason for freedom to take a mortal wound.

A voice was coming out of the amplifier, crackling across hundreds of miles of dark desert. *'Sidi bel Abbes receiving you . . . proceed with message.'*

Hugh Radford stifled a yawn of weariness and relief. Then he bent over the microphone to make his report.

We do hope that you have enjoyed reading this large print book.

Did you know that all of our titles are available for purchase?

We publish a wide range of high quality large print books including:
Romances, Mysteries, Classics
General Fiction
Non Fiction and Westerns

Special interest titles available in large print are:
The Little Oxford Dictionary
Music Book, Song Book
Hymn Book, Service Book

Also available from us courtesy of Oxford University Press:
Young Readers' Dictionary
(large print edition)
Young Readers' Thesaurus
(large print edition)

For further information or a free brochure, please contact us at:
Ulverscroft Large Print Books Ltd.,
The Green, Bradgate Road, Anstey,
Leicester, LE7 7FU, England.
Tel: (00 44) **0116 236 4325**
Fax: (00 44) **0116 234 0205**

Other titles in the
Linford Mystery Library:

DECEPTION

V. J. Banis

Playboy Danton Rhodes preys on rich women, squandering their fortunes before the inevitable divorce. He never expected to fall in love with Lois Carter, a married woman with a watertight prenuptial agreement; but when he learns that Lois's stepdaughter Dee needs to marry before her next birthday in order to receive her inheritance, Danton smells an opportunity. As Dee's cousin Helen arrives at the family home, she finds chaos — Lois has been violently attacked, and the suspect is none other than the familiar face she picked up along the way . . .

THE MAN ALL AMERICA HATED

Gordon Landsborough

In the aftermath of World War Two, Alec McCrae is the most hated American anywhere: he acted as intelligence officer for the Japanese and tortured American prisoners, sending thousands to forced-labour gangs. McCrae has managed to elude his pursuers for six years — but when he and his associates are finally exposed and confronted on a flight bound for Australia, he causes the plane to crash-land on a deserted Pacific island. And if the fugitives are to remain free, they will have to murder all the surviving crew and passengers . . .

SHADOW OF DOUBT

Mary Wickizer Burgess

A local woman suddenly takes on a new identity and goes on the run to another town. Meanwhile, Cathcart's respected district attorney, Turner Redland, is being threatened with blackmail for no discernible reason. Defense attorney Gail Brevard and her husband and law partner, Conrad Osterwitz, are drawn into the net. When a local con artist and possible witness turns up dead, there are plenty of suspects for the crime. Will Gail be able to make sense of it all in order to save the innocent and bring the guilty to justice?

KILL-BOX

Lawrence Lariar

When Private Eye Steve Ericson is asked by Dolly to keep an eye on her cheating husband Michael aboard the overnight Chicago-to-New York Express, it seems like a routine gig. But by the time the train rolls into Grand Central, the case has already gone off the rails: Michael is dead, causes unknown. Steve knows something is off-beat; anyone in the carriages could be involved — atomic scientists and beautiful women included. With the cops already eyeballing Dolly, Steve must clear her name — which wasn't all that untarnished to begin with . . .

DANGER IN NUMBERS

Noel Lee

When British pilot John Martin is involved in a dog-fight off the Scottish coast in his Hurricane aircraft, he sends his German opponent plunging to oblivion into the sea — but only at the cost of his own plane, which is fatally damaged. Sea winds carry his parachute inland, over rugged cliffs and coastline and finally over a former castle. Barely clearing the edge of the battlements, he lands jarringly on the roof. Unfortunately what appears to be a country home is actually the headquarters of a band of Nazi agents . . .

A GRAVE AFFAIR

Shelley Smith

When Edmund Burke, MP meets the woman he loves on a sunny afternoon, he cannot know that it is for the last time, or that a brilliant career is about to collapse in a scandal of murder and blackmail. Edmund, deep in negotiations that promise peace in the Middle East, is a target of nationalist fanatics who will stop at nothing to remove the main obstacle to their success. And he's about to discover where the loyalties of friends and family lie, as the police cast their net ever closer . . .